BLADE

Boston Rebels, book 5

RJ SCOTT

V.L. LOCEY

Love Lane Books

Copyright

Blade (Boston Rebels, 5)

Love doesn't have a formula. It's messy, unpredictable, and impossible to control for the autistic billionaire inventor and the hockey player who believes he's lost everything.

Moral "Dunny" Dunkirk has a passion for life. A robust outdoorsman, lover of life, and one of the Boston Rebels fan favorites, Dunny has always embraced excitement and the drive to try new things. During his inaugural flight behind the controls of a small plane, the fates decide to test his mettle in a way that he had never envisioned. When everything crashes down around him, he's lost in depression and alone in his cabin, facing an existence that is nothing like the one he previously led. Desperate to find some hope, Dunny reaches out to The Harvey Foundation who might be able to help, and he soon finds himself being lifted out of the pit of darkness he'd fallen into one shy uplifting smile at a time.

Accidental billionaire and inventor Cooper Harvey is happy in the seclusion of his lab, determined to make the world a better place. His autism gifts him with a unique vision but the media label him as quirky, reclusive, or a genius, and it's only in the most splendid isolation his vast wealth can buy that he feels safe. He goes out of his way to avoid sex with all its complicated and messy emotions, but a chance meeting with a test subject for his latest invention shakes his carefully controlled world. Interest in the hockey player who thinks he's lost everything shows Cooper that life can't be measured in chemical reactions, and attraction is unpredictable and messy. Terrified of facing something new, he doesn't know where to turn, but maybe if he's brave and with a partner who sees beneath the surface, he can finally find a love that makes sense.

https://rjscott.co.uk/read-blade

Dedication

To my family who accepts me and all my foibles and quirks. Even the plastic banana in my holster.
VL Locey

Always for my family.
RJ Scott

ROYAL LINES

BOSTON REBELS BOOK 4

RJ SCOTT & V.L. LOCEY

Love Lane Books

ONE

Cooper
_____

"I COULD MAKE YOU GO IN WITH ME IF I WANTED TO."

I caught my bodyguard's unwavering gaze in the mirror. As my personal security, Tony Avery, with his dubious past, was paid to be by my side whenever I left the CAHTech building. As his boss, he should do what I say, right? At least that was how I imagined it worked, but clearly, said dubious past made Tony unaware of official protocol.

"And again, I'm not coming in with you." Tony stared at me, and of course, it was me who backed down first.

"I could fire you," I mumbled to myself, forgetting my bodyguard had the hearing of a bat, the slyness of a fox, and the brawn of a huge fuck-off bear.

"You can't fire me when you didn't hire me."

I sat back in the seat with my arms crossed, daring anyone to make me get out of the car. I was safe in here and out there… well out there were people, and chaos, and me having to try my hardest to appear as if I wanted to be there.

"You need to get out of the car, sir." Tony added the *sir* with a forceful tone, and I winced.

"I like it in here," I defended. Hell, why anyone would want to leave this wonderfully safe, tricked out Escalade with its bomb-proof *this*, and its assassin-proof *that*, not to mention it's awesome refrigerator that held my Dr. Pepper and a cubby for my spare glasses and the softest buttery-leather seats was beyond me. It was safe inside here for a person who found the world too intimidating. In here, the only person I had to deal with was Tony, who understood me well enough to leave me alone and not expect me to be anything other than who I was. Outside the door was the rest of the world, and I didn't have much time for that. Besides, I'm one of the richest men in America, apparently, although I'd never counted all the money that seemed to pour into my company every time someone used Coopersil technology. So, being rich and all, I shouldn't have to get out of my car if I didn't want to. Right?

"I'm counting down from five, sir."

Jesus. "I'm not a child."

"Five."

"Tony, this is ridiculous—"

"Four."

"It's not like Uncle Jeremiah and Brianna will miss me if I don't go in—"

"Three."

"Why do I even have to do this? I visited last week—"

"It was a month ago. Also, two."

I curled my fingers around the handle and frowned at Tony's reflection. "I'm seriously going to get you fired."

"No. You're not. Also, one," Tony finished, and I heard the click of his locks and knew it would only be a matter of time before he opened the door and came to drag me out. I know I'm being overly dramatic, but I'd been dragged out of places before, and it was the worst thing ever for people to get so close and yank at me as if I didn't have a brain of my own.

"I don't want to do this," I said a little desperately as panic tightened my chest, and for a moment I thought Tony might give me an out; but no, he was exiting the car. "Okay! Okay, I'm going: I can get myself out!"

He raised a single eyebrow in answer. I cursed him under my breath, and then with one final inhale of the peaceful air back here, I opened my door and clambered out to stand under the awning attached to the side of Brianna's place. It wasn't safe for me to be dropped on the sidewalk. Apparently, death threats and money went hand in hand, so Brianna had deliberately built this space for me to go into the house. Also, I know that Tony would have done his due diligence, and I was safe, but this was the outside, and I felt vulnerable.

I didn't like the outside. Or people. Or actually anything messing with the flow of constant ideas fermenting in my brain. I didn't like the way people wanted to touch me or talk to me or ask me stupid questions about how I was or how I was feeling because I never knew the answers to any of that.

"Are you sure you're not coming in with me?" I asked Tony—the same as I did every four weeks when I had to get this thing done.

"Nope," Tony said without respect and tapped a unit in

the shotgun seat. "I have a hockey game to watch on this fancy-ass vid screen."

Oh, I could ask questions about this, and it would mean I could delay going in. "Who is playing this week?"

"Stop asking questions you have no interest in knowing the answers to and get inside."

"Is it the Boston Rabbles?" I could ask a ton of questions to avoid the inside of the sprawling house. "Are they playing the Raiders from, umm, Montreal, or something?" I knew very little about hockey-- only that it defied the laws of physics, and it was dangerous-- but I did know that Tony was a huge fan of the Boston team.

"*Rebels*, and it's the *Railers* from *Harrisburg*, and no they're not playing them; they're playing the Raptors from Arizona, and if you keep dithering and don't get yourself inside in the next ten seconds, I will carry you in."

The thought of big brawny Tony carrying me inside was scary, humiliating, and just a little bit sexy. Not that I thought Tony was sexy, but being carried was kind of sexy. Right? I mean, I don't exactly know much about sexy in all its variations, just that the infrequent porn I watch is split equally between straight and gay. Which I think might put me on the queer spectrum for sexual identity, but I never thought about it too much as I was already quite happy with my identity on the autistic spectrum. A brain way too fast for others, an accelerated academic life that had me graduating from MIT at nineteen, and then creating the magic-silver Coopersil fabric, meant instant millionaire status and expectations of more inventions, thus leaving no time for experimentation. Nor would it likely ever happen, unless I let in the messy world around me.

Nope. Not doing that.

"I'm going." I shut the door and straightened my shirt —the one that Tony had complimented the first time he took me to Brianna's house. It was the same shirt I wore every time I came here, and my pants were the standard black from the collection of forty that I chose from to wear each day. I probably needed a haircut, but I'd managed to force the loose waves into submission with some white goop that Brianna had ordered in for me, so I was what I imagined passed as presentable. I didn't much like the goop, but it held my hair in place, and it meant it didn't fall in my eyes when I was working. It was just one more sensory overload issue I had that I had to compromise with.

"Good luck to the Rabbles." I would use any excuse to avoid going inside, even hovering by the car door where Tony had lowered the window.

"Rebels."

"Why are they called that?"

Tony rolled his eyes, then made a move as if he was getting out, and I stepped back.

"You can tell me later," I said as if I wasn't trying to waste time, then walked to the back door without a backward glance. The door opened and there was Uncle Jeremiah, standing next to my PA Brianna. She was sixty-five, widowed, with two sons and a daughter, plus seven grandchildren, any of whom could be here today, and my uncle Jeremiah was her younger partner—sixty-one—with a shock of white hair.

Brianna got me to sign a contract saying I'd come to dinner at her house every fourth Sunday, and I only signed because she threatened to quit being my PA, and I had no idea how I'd handle things if she wasn't around. I mean, what kind of PA gets their boss to sign a legally binding contract to eat dinner with them? It didn't help that she was dating Uncle Jeremiah, who ran the charitable side of my company and was like a father to me. I try my hardest to be the best pseudo-son I can, within reason. However, I wasn't the best at getting around him either, and he was one-hundred-percent behind the official four-week visit.

"Hi, Coop." Jeremiah tugged me inside and hugged me, then it was Brianna's turn. I didn't mind them hugging me, in fact, I found them comforting—a safe place for me —and I never questioned it.

"Cooper." She kissed my cheek, not something she did in the office, then straightened my shirt and gave me a critical once-over. "You look tired."

"Are you supposed to say things like that to your boss?" I defended, and she smiled at me.

"No, but to a guest, yes, and only when it's true." We all headed for the vast kitchen at the center of the home, and I followed them like a duckling as Brianna summarized who was here—Brad, her eldest; and his wife, Chloe; and their three children, Zoe, Alex, and Connor. I pulled up everything I knew about Brad's little family. He was forty-three and worked in insurance. Chloe was forty-one and a part-time accountant who worked from home. Zoe was twelve, Connor eight, Alex three. I recalled Alex was still at the stage where he liked to throw food, and Zoe was learning how to play the piano. I didn't remember anything specific about Connor and, for a moment, I panicked, but it was too late to ask Brianna because suddenly we were in her kitchen, and they were all *there.*

"Hi, Mr. Harvey!" Zoe called from where she was nursing a mug of something at the kitchen table. It smelled like roast dinner in here, but I'm assuming she wasn't drinking that. I didn't ask.

"Midder Harvey!" Alex called.

I couldn't see Connor, but that didn't mean the middle sibling wasn't here, just that he was probably hiding, and I wondered momentarily whether he'd let me hide with him.

"Cooper." Brad shook my hand, and then Chloe bussed my cheek as we loosely side hugged. What I liked most about Brianna's extended family was that they didn't treat me as anything different, they just talked to me as if I fit in. And while I may not be an expert in being normal back, at least they didn't stare at me as if I had something on my face.

"Hello, how is everyone?" I asked generically and got a ton of information handed back to me.

"You know how it is." Brad rolled his eyes, much like Tony did to me.

"Good, always good." Chloe grinned so hard I wondered if she might hurt herself.

"I have pencils!" Alex waved them at me dramatically.

"My hands aren't big enough," Zoe mourned and tried to show me what she meant as she tapped out imaginary piano keys on the table.

"How about you?" Brad asked as he passed me a glass of water.

"I've just finished working on a nano-polymer-metal hybrid that's heading down to the development team," I announced. Brad nodded as if he completely understood what I meant. "I think they're hoping it will help amputees who need artificial limbs."

"So, it's got AI in it?" Brad asked.

"No, that would be stupid. It's like a metal." I waved away the rest of the explanation, and then, everyone was staring at me—or it felt that way. I'd fucked up again. Calling people stupid is wrong. "Excuse me, I need the bathroom."

I escaped quickly, weaving past Alex, who was throwing pencils on the floor, and headed out to the bathroom, which, on Sundays like this, was my sanctuary. I imagine that Brianna's family must think I have a problem with my bladder from the amount of times I need to use the facilities, but I know Jeremiah and Brianna both knew I needed space. However, this time, I didn't make it, seeing the middle sibling—Connor—peering out through the bannisters on the stairs.

"Hello," I said because I had the capacity to say that now, as I hadn't used that up on anyone else.

All Connor did was sniff and look even more miserable than he had before. Had I said something wrong? Maybe I'd misread the situation and saying hello had been deeply offensive.

"Are you okay?" I asked after a moment, and Connor sighed dramatically and slid down the stairs, tugging at his gold and black sports jersey that was way too big for him.

"I wanted to watch the afternoon hockey game, but Gramma wouldn't let me because it's Sunday and you're here."

"Oh." It seemed as if Connor was as pleased to be here

as I was. "Tony is watching the Rabbles in the car." Was that a helpful thing to say? Would the boy now want to go and sit in the car? Had I inadvertently started World War Three?

"Do you mean the Rebels?"

"I suppose I do."

"They're playing Arizona," Connor announced with another dramatic sniff. "And I don't think they'll win."

"Oh." Was this a serious thing?

"One of our wingers can't play."

"Oh. Who is that?"

He shrugged. "You don't know him."

He was right there. I didn't know anyone on the Rabbles—Rebels—by name, just that Tony was a big fan, and seemingly, so was Connor.

"I, umm… bathroom," I said and began to sidle away, and thankfully, Connor let me.

I didn't expect Uncle Jeremiah to be standing outside the bathroom when I was done wasting time, but there he was, arms folded over his chest, and no sign of little Connor anywhere.

"Can we talk?"

Oh God, that sounded ominous. The last time Jeremiah had said this was the New Year event of two thousand seventeen, and that was a memory I never wanted to relive. How was I to know that the woman in the elevator was going to jump on me as she did? It took me an entire minute of freaking out and attempting to fend her off, and thank God there'd been cameras in the space because I had all the evidence to back up my defense when she sued me for jumping *her*.

A very unpleasant experience altogether.

Jeremiah had asked me to talk back then. It hadn't been pretty when he spent an hour warning me of all the things that could go wrong for me if I didn't have my bodyguard with me when I was outside the lab. So, I guessed whatever he wanted to say now was another ominous discussion that I didn't want.

"Brianna told me you handed over your results on the hybrid material to the support team."

Huh? This was about work? "I did."

"The board has said you're to follow this one through to the end."

"Why would I do that?" I didn't want to disappoint the man who'd taken me in after my parents died, but he knew I wasn't the follow-through guy, I was the invent and pass on guy. I never understood why people wanted me to be involved in the products made from my materials because that was the boring part—I invent, and others make and sell, and that was it.

"Stock prices have... they need you to quash rumors that... you can be eccentric, but... we need to convey an emotional connection to... never mind." He straightened and placed a hand on my shoulder. "I worry about you."

"You don't need to. I'm happy doing what I do."

"But this new creation could lead to a huge change for a lot of lives."

"And that's good, but it doesn't need me working on it."

"You don't want even one syllable of praise or to see one moment of its application?"

I shrugged. Why did everyone else seem to need

praise? To me, it was just embarrassing, and I hated it. Hell, I didn't like it when people sang happy birthday to me either. "Not really."

He examined my face for a moment, and I thought maybe he wanted me to say something meaningful, only I couldn't think of anything to say. Then he pulled me into a tight hug, and I buried my face in his shoulder. I loved Jeremiah, he was always there for me, just like Brianna was as my PA, and Tony as my bodyguard.

"Love you, kid," he murmured.

"Love you too."

BY THE TIME I LEFT BRIANNA'S, MY SOCIAL WELL WAS empty, and I was never happier to be back in the car with Tony, who was suspiciously quiet.

"Did your team lose?" I asked as we joined the I-95 back into Boston.

"Yeah, five-one. Knew we would. It's not been the same since we lost Dunny. The balance is off, too few shots on goal. They'd better fix it soon, otherwise we might not even make the playoffs."

Oh, something I could comment on. I didn't get the rest, but if there was one thing I understood it was about balance in an equation where the number of atoms for each element in the reaction and the total charge is the same for both the reactants and the products so that the mass and the charge are balanced on both sides of the reaction.

"Maybe they need to fix themselves then," I suggested helpfully, but Tony sighed, and by the time I thought of something else I could say, we were back at the CAHTech Building on Stuart Street, and in no time at all, I was back in the peace and solitude of my apartment. The best bit about getting home from dinner at my PA's house with all her family was that I didn't need to do it for another three weeks and six days. The worst thing was that for a while after these visits, my private haven seemed so weird and empty, and it took me a while to find my equilibrium.

Brianna, Jeremiah, and Tony all said I needed more than work; said I needed a life, and love, and a family.

But I'm convinced they're all wrong.

WHEN I WOKE THE NEXT MORNING, I WAS BACK TO MY real life that ran exactly the way I wanted it. I stretched out to yoga, swam exactly eighty lengths under a beautiful blue Boston sky, shot ten baskets with a one-hundred-percent sink rate. After I showered and got dressed, I ate my usual breakfast of a bagel spread with cream cheese and admired the views from the patio over to the Charles River from the right front corner, and Boston Common on the left. I allowed myself fifteen minutes to gather my thoughts, then I headed down the back stairs to my laboratory on the floor below, which took up the vast majority of the twenty-fifth floor and was my happy place. I had a small office, which was all I needed given I had twenty-four other floors of people taking care of the two arms of CAHTech—the research side and the charitable side. The rest of my part was a closed-in sterile working space with large stainless-steel tables and as much equipment as I needed to do whatever my brain decided for the day.

I only shared this floor with Brianna's office, but as my PA, she was the dragon who guarded the space with a fierce protective eye, so no one ever disturbed me. I loved being isolated because I could think. In fact, the only person she let into this space was my uncle Jeremiah, and he knew never to interrupt me when I was in full flow.

This was why I was shocked when I opened the door to her office, intent on doing the polite thing and thanking her for dinner and company. I'd never done it before-- I usually sent flowers-- but today I felt as if I wanted to see her, which was wholly odd and pushed me right out of my comfort zone.

Only she wasn't alone.

And it wasn't my uncle in there with her.

It was two men—strangers—one tall strawberry-blond whose eyes widened in shock, and the other a mountain of a man with red hair and a scowl. They both stared at me and, if anything, the red-haired man-mountain with his gaze raking me from head to toe and back again, felt dangerous. Where was Tony? Why wasn't my bodyguard here saving me from whoever these strangers were on my floor? Both men had passes, and the taller, skinnier one was up on his feet with a broad grin and a hand extended to me.

Brianna smiled at me and stood from her seat. "Cooper, this is—"

"No," I stated and yanked the door shut between us, going back to my office and locking the door.

And hiding.

TWO

Moral

THE OLDER WOMAN IN THE FANCY GRAY SUIT BLINKED AT the door. Then, as quick as a sailfish, her composure returned, and she gave Phillippe, my brother, and me a professional smile. Cool, calm, and cautious.

"I'm sorry for that. Dr. Harvey isn't generally that averse to surprises." She flattened down her skirt and glanced at the door. I suspected she was covering up for the little man who had taken one look at me and run. Not that I blamed him. Lots of people had run away from me since the crash. Why should some skinny inventor, or whatever, be any different? "He probably forgot his glasses. He tends to leave them all over. I'll go fetch him. Just give me a moment."

"Of course," Phillippe said, rising as the lady had done. I stayed sitting. My crutches were on the other side of my brother's chair, just out of reach. Besides, she would be gone before I could hoist my ass out of my seat, then get the crutches under my arms. "We're happy to wait. Is that not right, Moral?"

"*Oui.* Yes," I replied woodenly. As if I had anywhere to go? This was the first trip from Vallée Rose, Québec, since I'd returned home from the hospital. I would not have even ventured from my cabin in the woods, if not for Phillippe forcing me. Literally, he heaved me out of my chair at home and wrangled me into his new SUV, his wife tossing clothes into a bag as my brother and I wrestled. Before, I could have easily taken him down, but now... now I was weak from my hospital stay, my body covered with healing scars and trauma that I feared I would never recover from. Between my brother and his tiny wife, Yuka, they'd shoved me into the Forester and off we drove. Flying was out of the question. The nightmares of that day woke me nightly still. Another thing that might never go away, I was afraid.

She nodded, then scurried out of the massive meeting room.

"The man had glasses on his face," I pointed out. My brother shrugged. "This is a waste, Phillippe." I shifted in the padded seat, the back of the cushion digging into the tender flesh where the staples had recently been removed.

"Stop being so negative, Moral. Nothing is a waste if it brings hope."

Hope. Yes, well that was something I had lost the moment I came to, after several days in a coma, to discover that I had -- somehow, and miraculously, according to my sister-in-law -- survived the crash of my new single-engine plane. I was more a Frankenstein monster now, as opposed to a hockey player. Scars riddled my body, one along my hairline that stood out brightly where they had shaved my hair to stitch my scalp back together. I was a ghoulish collection of missing limbs, screws, bolts, and staples.

"As you say." I sighed, twisting in my chair to alleviate the pressure on the back of my stump. My eyes skimmed over the artwork on the walls, soft voices leeching through the closed door Miss Brianna had exited through, to a solid wall of glass. The Boston skyline lay before me. Something that I knew as well as I knew all the paths to and from my log cabin back home. I'd played here for years, lived here in a spacious apartment just down the street from Fenway Park. Now, this city felt like a nightmare of places that I couldn't access without considerable hassle, either with crutches or in that damn wheelchair. My sight caught a glint of silver in the bright fall sky. A plane coming into Logan Airport. The low hum of voices faded away as I fixated on the jumbo jet growing closer and closer.

VALLÉE ROSE TOWER, I AM HAVING TROUBLE WITH MY engine…

My sight flickers to the smoke pouring from the nose of the single engine plane. My heart is lodged in my throat, thundering madly, on this my third solo flight after receiving my private pilot license. What a miserable joke fate is. A trio of flights, then I die. Alone. No husband or wife or children to mourn me. Only Phillippe, Yuka, and Penelope. Who would feed Penelope? Phillippe would. He would care for my dog. Thank the heavens for my sibling. He would care for my beloved basset hound.

Vallée Rose Tower, I am having trouble with my engine.

The reply is unintelligible. I try again in French. Still garbled. My mouth is so dry; the plane is losing altitude steadily; my palms slick with sweat.

Vallée Rose Tower, I am having trouble with my engine. Please reply.

Please. Please. Please reply. The ground is coming closer and closer. Please reply!

Foxtrot Michael Dundee Paul, roger.

Oh God, thank you! Thank you so much oh mighty God!

Foxtrot Michael Dundee Paul, can you make a right base for runway two? Can you see it? Do you have that in sight?

My eyes scan the land hurtling upward.

Non, Vallée Rose Tower, I cannot see the runway. I am not going to make it. I'm not going to—

"Moral. Moral!" Strong hands gripped my shoulders and shook gently, snapping the hold the memory had on me. My eyes, which are now seeing my brother's worried face, instead of the Canadian wilderness hurtling up to meet me, skitter around the room. Sweat runs down the back of my neck as my lungs stop seizing. Yes, yes, we are in Boston. At the tall tower that holds what my brother, my physical therapist, and my mental health counselor all believe to be my return to being able-bodied. "Moral, are you here with me now?"

"Yes, yes, I'm here. Sorry. I just..." I chanced a look at

the skyline. The jet, now long gone, probably landed safely at Logan as hundreds of thousands of planes do every year. Millions perhaps. My shoulder aches. Wincing at the pressure on the reconstructed shoulder joint, I let out a shaky breath. "I saw a plane in the sky. Stupid I know."

He leaned in to kiss my damp brow. We've always been affectionate like that. Mama and Papa were that way. Always hugging and kissing me and my younger brother, each other, the dogs, the cats, friends, strangers. They were incredibly demonstrative. I missed them both so much.

"It is not stupid. It's PTSD, which is very normal after a traumatic experience. Your counselor told you so many times." I shrugged my good arm, moving around in my seat to ensure I can't see the damn window anymore. "It will pass as time goes by. Once you're back on your feet." His eyes flared. "I mean when you're recovered. I'm sorry. That was—"

"It was fine. A saying. Someday, yes, I will be back on my foot." My sight touched on my lower half, the left leg so strong and thick, powerful from skating. Then the right, gone below the knee, my trouser leg pinned up neatly by my brother just this morning. Phillippe wasn't amused. "It was a joke. I'm a joker, right?"

"You don't have to pretend, Moral," he said before patting my cheek and returning to his seat. "And you will return to your life fully within a year or two, with lots of therapy and this new prosthetic alloy that Dr. Harvey is creating. When you're sad, be sad. When you're happy, be happy. I'm not the little boy who lost his parents and had to rely on you and Aunt Celeste to care for him. I'm twenty-six now."

"Yes, and now you're taking care of me. Isn't life funny?" I asked, but there was no humor in the question. "We should just go home. I don't think this experimental bullshit is for me, Phillippe. I have too much therapy to get through..."

He was about to argue, as he did, the stubborn ass, when the door opened and the older woman returned with the reluctant looking man who had bolted what seemed like hours ago. A glance at my watch showed it had only been five minutes since the brilliant inventor with the wide brown eyes had left in such a hurry. I nudged Phillippe and jerked my scruffy chin at my crutches. He hurried to comply, passing the crutches over, then reaching to help me out of the chair. I shot him a scowl. My brother lowered his hands to let me struggle upward. It didn't go well with a healing shoulder and only one leg. Embarrassed at my weakness, I grunted at my brother in French, a quick request for aid. He whispered something back in our native tongue that was not complimentary as he levered me up to my feet. The doctor looked up at me as I wobbled around on my crutches, his dark eyes growing even wider behind his glasses as I got to my full height. Balanced now, I offered him my hand.

He seemed reluctant to take it, but after a slight poke from Miss Brianna, he clasped my fingers, gave them a quick pump, and then dropped them.

"Good afternoon, Dr. Harvey. Thank you for seeing us," Phillippe said jovially, the greeting obviously forced. There was nothing cheerful about this meeting. "My brother, Moral, and I are thrilled to have this time with you. Your personal assistant assured us that you would love to hear my brother's story. That it would help in your creation of this new metal for athletic prosthetics. Were we not understanding the reply to our email?"

"Your email," I muttered in French. Phillippe shot me a glare.

Dr. Harvey and Miss Brianna had exchanged a rather poignant look. Perhaps this famous inventor had no more interest in being here than I did. He certainly seemed anxious, his fingers working his skinny tie or tugging on one of his pecan-colored curls.

"I, umm… it's fine. Totally fine. We can talk. Sorry about your accident." Dr. Harvey made a vague gesture to my leg, then my forehead.

His gaze warmed some as he studied my face. As I looked down at the floor, I wished the man had been a little less attractive. I'd always had a thing for slim little men that I could pick up and cuddle. I also liked petite women. My brother liked to say that my frame had to be so big to contain all the affection I had for life, people, and animals. Sadly, my love of life and living it was no more. All the passion had been lost when the surgeons sawed off my leg. I was a man with no future. All the things that I had loved were gone now. Hockey, driving, running, bicycling, canoeing, hunting, fishing, boating. How could I ever do any of those things with one leg? Depression had taken root in my soul and, while I could call it out, I had no idea how to exorcise the sadness.

"Thank you," I finally said after getting a look from Phillippe. "I will be dancing soon they tell me in therapy."

Everyone smiled uncomfortably. Phillippe finally spoke up.

"Of course you will." He clapped my back, taking care to avoid the shoulder surgery site.

"Although my dance moves were not good before," I tossed out glibly, then forced a laugh. Dr. Harvey stared up at me as if trying to work out why I was chuckling about a near-death experience. I had no clue why I was. Because it was what Dunny did, yes? He joked; he laughed; he lived life to the fullest. Moral had to allow Dunny out regularly or people would suspect how deep I had sunk into the pit of sadness. "Can we sit now? My armpits are sore. This city is not always kind to people with issues." I couldn't say disabilities. It was too permanent. Too scary. Too forever.

"Yes, of course."

We all sat down. Miss Brianna and Phillippe started talking. Dr. Harvey and I sat silently, him fiddling with his blue framed glasses or his curls as he stared openly at me while I kept my sight locked on where my leg used to be. It ached at times. How bizarre was that? How could something that was not there give me pain? Regina, my physical therapist back home, said it was a common thing. They call it phantom pain and it usually goes away after several months, but can linger for years. It was not mental as they once thought, but real sensations taking place in the brain and spinal cord.

"How did you lose your leg?" Dr. Harvey asked out of the blue, startling not only me, but Phillippe and Miss Brianna from their discussion.

"A plane crash," I replied, my throat dry suddenly. I willed the creeping sense of a flashback away by fixating on his face. It was a curious face with big, bright, inquisitive eyes, a slim nose, and pink lips. He was pale, his cheeks covered with new whiskers.

"What was the cause?" He leaned in closer, the smell of his aftershave now tickling my nose. It was a brisk scent, manly, clean. Pleasant. "Weather related? Did you hit a bird? You're from Canada, correct? Your accent is nice. Did you run into a Canada goose?"

"Faulty fuel selector valve, they think," I replied, eyeing him with some interest. "Do you think that the only birds we have in Canada are geese?"

He sat back, blinking as if taken off guard. "Well, no, of course not. I'm quite aware of the vast multitude of birds that inhabit Canada, including loons, various breeds of ducks, grouse, pheasant, songbirds, gray jays -- which I believe are the official bird -- as well as falcons, hawks, bald eagles, owls, and goshawks. I only mentioned Canada geese as they're the famed cause of the airstrike that resulted in Flight 1549 crash landing in the Hudson River on January 15, 2009. Captain Chesley 'Sully' Sullenberger was able to pull off a very risky water landing, saving all one hundred fifty souls with only a few serious injuries."

"Umm, yeah." I had no clue what to do with all that information other than agree.

"Tom Hanks played Captain Sullenberger in the movie titled *Sully*. It was quite good. I enjoy everything Tom Hanks does. So, it was not pilot error or any other natural phenomenon. Interesting. Do you happen to know how many times a fuel selector valve malfunctions in small planes?"

"Umm, no?" He was such an odd duck. Cute, but odd, and it seemed as if he really was the eccentric and reclusive inventor the media made him out to be. He wouldn't quite meet my eyes, and he was constantly moving the fingers of his right hand to tap his thumb.

"Oh, that's too bad. I'll look into it. If there is a preponderance of issues with that type of valve, perhaps it should be brought to the FAA or their counterpart in Canada, which would be the TCCA."

"Yes, well, okay. Yes, that would be good?" I glanced at Phillippe, who was looking just as confused as I felt.

"Excellent. I'll look into it and get back to you," Dr. Harvey said, rose, and stuck his hand outward. As I shook it, I took note of how soft his fingers and palm were in comparison to mine. "I'll let you know my findings."

"Dr. Harvey," Phillippe interjected as he made a beeline for the door. I heard the doctor exhale before turning to look at us. "What about my brother's situation? Can your new discovery help him return to the NHL? Go back to being a skater?"

The doctor pushed his glasses up his nose. "He was a professional athlete, right?" We both nodded. "No." That seemed blunt, but I wasn't stupid. I'd already come to that conclusion on my own. "But he *will* be able to skate, run, and drive one day."

"Will I be able to dance?" I asked to break the gloom that his blunt reply had brought into the room. He stared at me, blinked, and then just as I opened my mouth to explain I was joking, he smiled. It was an adorable, awkward, off-kilter smile that lit up his face.

"Jokes. I like them. Where do one legged dancers go for breakfast? I-Hop." His PA and my brother gasped. I gaped for a moment, then broke up, my laughter rolling out of me like a dam bursting. Dr. Cooper Harvey grinned at me, the tips of his ears turning pink. "I'm sorry. Was that not an acceptable pun? I have autism if you didn't already know, and sometimes I get my social cues mixed up." I'd read the most recent article in the *Times* about the doctor, Bill Gates, and other brilliant men. It stated their brains were wired differently. I got that—my brain is wired for hockey.

Fuck. What would I do with that brain now?

"It was a perfect joke. Thank you." I wanted to hug him, but I clung to my crutches instead, using the back of my hand to wipe away the tears of mirth when necessary. I'd not laughed since the day my plane had gone down.

He nodded, spun, and made his getaway, pausing only a second to peek back over his shoulder at me before closing the door. Miss Brianna started making apologies for Dr. Harvey's lack of etiquette. I waved off her worry. I'd enjoyed meeting the man. He'd managed to tug me from my own misery with his scientific ramblings, straightforward talk, and shy smile. He'd made me laugh with his bluntness and the joke. I'd not thought I would ever do that again. If he could do that for me, maybe… just maybe… his magic metal leg would also be able to perform some sort of miracle.

THREE

Cooper

WHERE DO ONE LEGGED DANCERS GO FOR BREAKFAST?

Did I really just say that? To an amputee? To an amputee who, despite the lack of his lower leg and the fact he was on crutches, could probably crush me like a grape? I think maybe I crossed a line again.

"Cooper, we need to talk," Brianna said from outside my office door, but I ignored her. The door was locked anyway, so she couldn't come in. "Cooper *Alexander* Harvey, I won't say it again."

I hated when she pulled out the big guns and called me by my full name. It didn't happen often, but when it did, I felt the same as that confused kid who'd ended up at Uncle Jeremiah's place with his belongings in a duffle. My hold on today was loosening, my thoughts unraveling, and my happy, peaceful place was gone. Partly because I'd been dragged into a meeting I hadn't known about, and partly because somehow the big redheaded man had intimidated the life out of me, and I'd made a joke that wasn't appropriate. I stared at my knuckles, white as I gripped my desk, and counted back from twenty, attempting to settle my breathing, but nothing was working. Now was not the time for a panic attack, or to vanish up to my apartment for three days and avoid all human contact. Both things were on my to-do list whenever I was out of control.

"I told you that the board wanted you to have a front facing project." She sighed. "I gave you months of notice on that and put today's meeting in your journal. Did you even look at your journal today?"

I glanced at the heavy tome sitting on the edge of my desk, close to falling to the floor. Sometimes the thing would be full to bursting with my ideas, and doodles, and colored tape demarcated each subject, and I even drew tiny ladybugs as bullet points. Other times, the days were empty as I failed to connect to what others called *real life*. On those days, I didn't find a happy medium.

"Check your journal," Brianna prompted, and I released my grip on the desk and reached for the leather-bound story of my life, touching the worn outside, and then yanking my hand back as if it had burned me.

"It's not in there," I lied just loud enough so she'd hear. I didn't want to open today's page because I didn't have the energy to meet the challenge of a blank page.

"I'm coming in," Brianna murmured, and I heard the beeping as she entered her code and the door swung open. "Hi," she said in her most careful and gentle tone. She and Uncle Jeremiah were the only people with the code—the only two that I allowed into the room because they knew me, and my ups and downs, and didn't judge me for any of it. Oh, and Tony, of course, but he would only come in here to rescue me from assassins, alien invasion, or zombie attacks—his words, not mine.

"I made a joke about hopping," I blurted miserably.

"Yes, you did." Brianna crossed over to the desk and picked up the journal, flipping to today's date and turning it to show me that yes, the appointment was in there, if only I'd been on a good day and thought to check. Too many other things fought for brain space, and I was so close to the beginning stage in a brand-new experiment that real life was just something that got in the way.

"Why the hell did I make that joke?"

"It was a funny joke, and Mr. Dunkirk seemed to agree, so don't be too hard on yourself."

My skin felt hot, and I rested my forehead on the cool desk. "Stupid joke in front of him," I muttered and banged my head gently three times.

"Don't do that, sweetheart," Brianna admonished with love and used a strong touch to sit me back in my chair, then smoothed my head where I'm sure it's red. "I think it went very well, and they were more than happy when they left."

"They've gone now?"

"Yes."

A small part of my tension unwound, and when that happened, it caused a cascade in my thoughts, and I began to relax. There must be a thousand people working in this building, but none of them were strangers allowed onto the floor below this one.

"You'd better start at the beginning," I said, after one

last drawn-out sigh. I needed complete information, which would make me feel more in control. I did have a memory of concerns from the board suggesting I was maybe losing touch with my end user. Whatever that meant. All I know is that money drove the board, and I was basically their cash cow, and they needed me to perform, which was difficult when my inner narrative failed to help me understand the situations they put me in.

Brianna scribbled some details into my journal, leaving room for me to add my doodles if I wanted to, and passed it back to me.

"I'll get you some lunch." She patted my shoulder and left. I closed my eyes for a moment, relishing the silence of my room, and then with determination I opened the journal, read the notes, and launched a browser to research. There was a warren of information, and when I came out the other end, the sandwich and chips at my side were untouched, and my coffee was cold.

MY WATCH VIBRATED. LOST AS I WAS IN FORMULAS AND outcomes, it took me a while to realize why it was tapping a rhythm against my wrist. I blinked at it as my thoughts refocused, and then all the other things I needed to focus on began to filter back in.

Moral Dunkirk, twenty-nine years old, six foot four inches in height, two hundred twenty-five pounds of muscle, shoots right, and drafted in the fifth round after graduating from Université du Québec à Trois-Rivières after four years of playing collegiate hockey for the school hockey team, the Patriotes. Thirty-first pick. Plays center but also can play either wing position, winner of the NHL Plus-Minus once. Plus-minus is a stat used to determine how often a player is on the ice when a goal is scored for the team versus against the team. Also, a two-time recipient of the Lady Byng Memorial trophy for exhibiting the best kind of sportsmanship and gentlemanly conduct combined with showing a high standard of playing ability and was fit and healthy, albeit now an amputee after the plane he was piloting had a one in a million issue.

There wasn't much in the way of detail about the crash itself, other than the tabloid garbage that I tended to avoid since they used lazy journalism and often mislabeled me as eccentric, or in some cases, weird. Like they even knew me at all! The crash had been brutal—it had to have been for Mr. Dunkirk to lose his leg like he did—and it didn't sit well with me when I watched footage of hockey and saw the way he moved across the ice as graceful as… well, as something that was graceful. From a purely physical point of view, he was a masterpiece of engineering, his lower body strength phenomenal, his explosive skating was something to behold. He was broad chested, tall even out of skates, and he was utterly determined.

A perfect physical sample, and exactly the right person for the trial.

We'd be lucky to have him—if he wasn't ready to run in the opposite direction as soon as he saw me—at least that is what the board told me, whose missive was handed to me with caution from Brianna and forced enthusiasm from Uncle Jeremiah. At least they didn't suggest I go to any meetings with them because there are only so many complimentary jellybeans I can put in order of color before I get bored.

Sometimes I rue the day that I invented Coopersil. Yes, it had saved lives but discovering the chemical reactions I did, it had forced me out of the obscurity I wanted and into a spotlight I hated.

I rolled my neck, relaxing each tense muscle, pasted a smile on my face, and opened the door to Brianna's office. I could see her through the glass to a well-equipped kitchen beyond, making coffee, and saw the brothers were in the middle of a heated debate in low tones filled with temper, completely in French, so involved that they never noticed me at the door. French-Canadian had its own specific cadence, but I knew more than enough French to get the gist of what they were saying, and they were saying a lot.

"I don't want to be a lab rat," Moral snapped.

"But what if you get to skate again?"

"Who says I even want that?!"

"I know you want to skate again. Jesus, Moral—"

"Why? Because you tell me that's what I want?"

"No, because you're born to be on the ice."

"Like a child with one of those penguins going round and round in circles."

"No, there are options. Look, you could coach, or work with a sled team, you could—"

"This is not meant to be my life." Moral waved at his knee and added a curse.

"Moral, I get how you feel, but—"

"How can you know how I feel?! Come back to me when you lose your leg, and we can talk about what I might be feeling!" Moral's eyes widened as he finished. "Shit! I'm sorry!" And he slumped in his seat, even as Phillippe seemed to curl in on himself. Was now a good time to clear my throat and announce my appearance?

"Hello," I said instead, and both men moved in their chairs to face me. Phillipe scarlet faced and Moral a lot slower and looking so defeated I wanted to tell him I would fix everything.

Because yes, that was where my stupid brain was taking me.

I knew I shouldn't have spent so long watching the Boston Rebels behind-the-scenes documentaries where Moral declared his love for classic books and cars and outdoor adventures and said his idea of heaven was a week in the woods.

After watching the Rebels play—at least I got their name right now—who could have known that a hockey player as intense as he was, with all his crashing around and checking other skaters, could have a sensitive side.

He also said he loved dogs and owned a basset hound called Penelope. I don't have a pet because they would just be all over my experiments and would need me to remember to feed them, but if I was to choose a pet, it would be a cat over a dog one-hundred-percent of the time.

Phillipe rose to his feet. I noticed Moral had his crutches right next to him this time and seemed to be less wobbly as he stood. It had only been a few days since we last met, so I doubt he'd healed any more, but he was probably more confident is all.

"Dr. Harvey," Phillipe said and extended his hand again, which I shook, followed by Moral, who nodded as we clutched hands.

By this time—thankfully—Brianna was back with a tray of coffee and snacks, and I dived straight in for the only mini Milky Way bars on the plate, my absolute favorite, already unwrapping it before realizing everyone was staring at me.

"Brain fuel," I announced, as if that explained everything. "Did you hear about the candy vehicles from another planet?"

The brothers blinked at me, and Brianna rolled her eyes.

"No," Moral said after no one answered me.

"In England, Milky Way bars are different and these ones here, with the caramel, are called Mars Bars, so you have to know that for the joke to make sense." I waited for the nods of understanding—I would hate for no one to get the joke I was making up.

"Go on…" Moral encouraged.

"Well, candy vehicles from another planet are Mars Bars Mars Cars," I finished and waved what was left of my chocolate. At first, no one laughed, and then Moral let out a snort that turned to a chuckle.

"Do you have jokes for everything?" He smiled at me, and the smile reached his eyes. I think he was relaxing.

"People who tell jokes are consistently rated as more confident." I gave my usual reply, and he nodded as if that made perfect sense.

"You don't seem like you should lack confidence," Moral pointed out, and I melted at the way his accent softened his words. I hadn't realized that the French-Canadian accent would make me all fuzzy inside, but clearly it did. "With all of this, I mean." He waved at the office, but I know he was indicating the entire building, from basement parking to roof, all of it owned by me. I should tell him now that this wasn't just offices and laboratory space, but my fortress. However, I couldn't think of a humorous, or at least vaguely non-serious, way of telling him.

"Anyway, about your leg," I began bluntly, then sucked spots of chocolate from my thumb.

"Me... my... umm..." Moral cleared his throat and Phillipe elbowed him. "Yes, my leg, or my lack of leg. Shit, sorry, gallows humor. So yes..."

For the first time since I met him, Moral seemed flustered, and I wondered if my Mars Bar Mars Car joke was too bad because I couldn't think what else might be making him weird. I guess it must be the money thing.

"I'm no different from you," I announced as I sat down. "Just ignore all of this," now it was my turn to wave at the office and the building, "and let's get down to business. First up, I've measured the lower basement space, and I think we can fit a rink one-fifty by seventy, so not full size, but I think that will be enough to work with."

"Sorry?"

I looked up from my notes. "Is that not big enough? Maybe I need to rethink."

"I can't even... you're building a rink... in your basement?"

"Well, it's given over to parking right now, but since

we have company sponsored rideshare programs it's never used, so it makes sense."

"It makes sense to build a rink in your building?"

"Absolutely. If we're testing and working hypothesis, we will need baseline and regression analysis, and we—"

"A rink," Moral repeated, and I realized this was clearly a sticking point.

"Yes. A rink. An oval," I peered at my notes, "with lines, and a wall, and netting, although I'm not sure we'll need the plexiglass as part of it will be right up against a wall. Never mind, we'll cross that bridge when we come to it. Also, we'll create an apartment for you on this floor, not my floor."

"An apartment? But I have an apartment, my own apartment."

Glancing up at him, I saw his eyes were narrowed. His brother stared at me like I had chocolate around my mouth. I bent my head as if I was checking my notes and furtively wiped my finger across my lips, just in case.

"He has an apartment," Phillipe added. "With a gym, and the Rebels are working on his rehab right now."

"Absolutely, but I suggest it would be the ideal situation for you, and your brother if he so wishes, to stay here for the time of your rehab and during the trial. We have PT on staff, as well as a psychologist, plus several counselors, and of course, the experiments can be efficiently evaluated in a controlled environment."

"I'm not a lab rat," Moral countered defensively.

"Of course you're not. I'm just suggesting a suitable location in which to help you regain some kind of normality, albeit limited, and for us to learn from your journey. Isn't that what you want as well?"

Moral's expression was suddenly bleak, then in a flurry of movement he stood with his crutches and went to the door.

"That's the definition of a lab rat, and worse, it's one who doesn't have any hope," he said flatly.

And then he left.

FOUR

Moral

I'D ALWAYS THOUGHT BETTER AT THE BARN.

Back in the day—when I was able-bodied—being on the ice was like a kind of therapy for me. Even as a kid, when it was me and Phillippe playing shinny games behind the house, mindfulness was always easiest found with cold air in my face and the steady sluice-sluice-sluice of sharp blades on frozen water.

It seemed those days were gone. Perhaps it was too early for this. I should have protested more when the Rebels organization had first floated the idea of this absurd night. Phillippe had thought it a good idea, as did Yuka and Aunt Celeste. Even my therapist back home had signed off on it, citing that it would be good for me to have closure. I was in the sky box with the owner, the mayor of Boston, and one of the esteemed senators from Massachusetts, but being here didn't feel like a good idea. My teammates— oops, no, my bad—my *ex*-teammates and the opposing team from Philly were down on the ice watching the large screen display over center ice, and none of this felt right.

My tie felt too tight, my lungs too small, my skin crawling with ants. My sight darted from the screen -- where various clips from my all too short career with the Rebels were playing -- to the SRO crowd to my brother looking so proud. I couldn't quite bring myself to look at the clips of my younger days, the goals that I had scored, the hits that I'd delivered. That man on the skates was not me. Not anymore. That was pre-crash Moral. The guy who embraced life, lived it at high speed, and never once looked back to see the grim reaper on his heels. I drove fast cars, loved faster men and women, boated, swam, hunted, fished, ran marathons, and biked through the Canadian Rockies just last summer with Marquis and Xander. That Moral played a contact sport that he loved. That man was no more.

I was now post-crash Moral. A man covered in scars, filled with refurbished parts, and missing a limb. The five minutes that the team had given me came to an end. Everyone in the arena was on their feet, the applause deafening, and the chants of "Dun-nee! Dun-nee! Dun-nee!" rattled off the metal I-beams far above. A spotlight hit me. I wasn't prepared for this. Not emotionally, and certainly not physically.

"Let me help you," Phillippe whispered as everyone in the owner's box stood and clapped. I shook off his hand and fumbled with my crutches until I had them settled. Then, I rose like a wobbly elk calf freshly born. The cheers grew louder. They all thought I was so brave. What a hero I was. How amazing that through sheer will and that streak of Quebecois stubbornness, I had survived a horrid crash. What a miracle it was! What a pity about his leg, but he would find something else to fill his life for the next fifty or so years! Dunny would never be forgotten. But I would. The team was subtly easing me off the roster and away from the fans. Slowly, yes, and with great sympathy and empathy, but Nick Sinclair already had my resignation letter on his desk. My agent had signed off on it. It was a done deal. We all knew that I was never coming back. Even if, through the sheer grace of God or some wide-eyed inventor, I did get back on skates, it would only be for my own enjoyment. Maybe I could play on a sled team somewhere, perhaps for my country in the Paralympics at some point, but my NHL career was now over. This little ceremony was the first of many bittersweet ways the team and I were parting ways. It hurt more than any injury I had sustained in that damned crash.

I smiled and waved a hand, trying to look like the courageous man the papers and, yes, the team, had painted me to be. Deep inside, I was anything but fearless. I was sad. And defeated. And if there had not been glass here, I might have thrown myself over the side just to end the misery and lingering pain.

"Excellent ceremony!" Nick shouted to be heard over the thumping music now filling the barn. My little homage was over. The boys were ready to play. That, as they say, was that. The fat lady had just sung. I nodded dully at Nick, easing myself back into my front row seat. A server hustled over, a pretty young woman wearing a gold vest and black slacks, with a tray of champagne in her hands. She glanced at me, at the scars on my face, and looked away.

"Thank you, but no," I told her. I was taking too many

meds to drink. And, in all honesty, I feared that if I did start drinking, I would never stop. "Some orange soda, please."

She nodded, eyes averted, as Nick and the senator took a flute of bubbly. Phillippe removed his jacket, smiling at me over his glass of lemon-lime soda, and let his attention fall back to the game. I did the same, easing my weight up a bit to take the pressure off my stump where it rested on the seat.

The senator, an older woman with glasses and short gray hair cut into a fashionable bob, placed her hand on my arm. I pulled my gaze from the faceoff to look at her.

"I'd just like to say that we're all so impressed with how valiantly you've battled back from your injuries. If you'd be willing to someday come to my office in Washington, I would love to sit down with you to discuss how to make more improvements to the handicapped access areas in our major cities. I know that we're doing a good job, but there is always room for improvement."

"We're hoping that Moral will not be in a wheelchair for long," Phillippe piped up.

I let him talk to the senator for me. He had become quite good at being my mouthpiece. For someone who had been so loud and rambunctious at one time, I now found myself happiest when I could just be left alone. Yuka called it moping. Perhaps it was, but it was where I felt the most comfortable. People were always pushing me to be cheery or upbeat. Thanking whatever gods they worshipped for sparing me, or giving me strength. I wondered why their gods had let me fall to the ground like a stone. Why had the Lord thought that ending my career and battering my body so badly that I nearly died was a good thing? It was a severe crisis of faith—even a dumb hockey player like me could figure that out without the help of clergy—as well as a severe case of post-traumatic depression.

While my brother and the senator talked about issues for people like me, I watched the game. Marquis was on fire tonight. Obviously, his love affair with Prince Kaleb was lifting his spirits, as well as his game. His passes were crisp, tape-to-tape passes that got the Rebels off to an early lead with a beautiful tic-tac-toe passing sequence between himself and Austin Rowe, who had been shuffled up to take my place as center on the second line. The kid had a keen eye and that Rowe speed. Teaming him up with Marquis had been a brilliant coaching move. Rowe simply flipped the pass that he'd gotten from Marquis over the glove side of the Philly goalie and the red light flashed. The crowd went wild, and the Rebels goal song filled the air. I smiled wistfully, remembering when that was me down there sneaking a puck past a tendie, feeling the rush of the hometown love, and having a celly in the corner with my teammates.

"Your soda, sir." I glanced up at the server. She still could not look me in the face.

"Thank you," I whispered, taking the glass of fizzy orange pop from her.

She skittered off. I let out a sigh that my brother didn't miss. He cocked an eyebrow at me as he continued relaying my struggles with narrow passageways and the difficulty of using public transit. Not that I had even tried to get onto a train or bus after my one misadventure trying to go shopping by myself one day after we'd arrived in Boston. I'd only wanted to pick up some razors while my brother napped after a long drive. I'd gotten myself to the train depot, but the gap was too wide for me to roll into the train. That was yet another lesson on how difficult it was for people with disabilities to do the daily errands we all take for granted. Using the crutches for that long of a walk would have been painful to the extreme. The crutches worked up blisters on my hands, and made my arms and new shoulder ache when I overused them.

"Nice goal!" Nick cheered on my right. His smile was wide until he turned to me then it slipped a bit. That happened quite a lot. People didn't quite know how to talk to me now that I was different. "So hey, when you're on your feet again—fuck. Sorry, I didn't mean it like that."

Where do one legged dancers go for breakfast? I-Hop.

That made me smile. Cooper didn't seem to be the least bit affected by my new state. I liked that. I liked it a lot. He didn't look at my scars or that dangling pant leg with remorse or unease. He treated me like he seemed to treat everyone. Hell, he even told jokes. No one else, not even my brother, who had teased me unmercifully for all his twenty-six years on this planet, joked with me. Not anymore. Maybe I needed to be around more people like Dr. Cooper Harvey.

"It's okay," I assured the man who used to own my contract. Well, still did, for another week, then my agent would make a blanket social media post about my retirement from the game. "What were you going to say?"

A greasy goal for the Rebels stalled the conversation for a minute. I watched the replay on the wall-mounted

TVs. Xander and two Philly defenders had been creating all kinds of chaos in front of the away team's net. Joachim took a wobbly shot from the blue line that bounced off the left pad of Lars Milquist, the Philadelphia goalie. The puck dropped to the ice and the goalie tried to cover it up, but it slipped free. Xander, Joachim, and one of our D-men gathered in front of the net, poking and jabbing at the puck as the goalie fell to his side in a mad attempt to block his net. Two big defenders began shoving at the Rebels, jabbing at their tendie. Joachim shoved the puck between the wickets of the Philly goalie. The linesman behind the net immediately pointed at the puck resting just behind the goalie and well over the line. The goal horn sounded and the red light flashed. Nice. So damn nice. Fuck, but I wanted to be down there with my friends. It hurt deep down in my soul not being able to thump Joachim on his head or reach out to fist bump the goal scorer and his linesmen as they skated past the bench.

"The boys are looking good tonight!" Nick hooted. The others in the box agreed, then fell back into conversation. "So, like I was saying, once you're ready, I got a lead on a sled team that's setting up here in Boston. New league, we're backing them, community support and all that. Should be a worthwhile venture, if you'd like to play, or maybe even coach. 'Course if you're not interested in that, we can always find you a spot in management. Guy with your skills and knowledge of the game? Shit, we can put you in any upper management department. Player development is always looking for guys like you. Or you could be a European scout! Lots of travel, which is great for a single guy. Get to pick out the best of the best of the upcoming crop of kids across the pond. Or I could talk with Dell Matthews of North American scouting, or we could tap Mickey Rogers in the NCAA scouting office. Lots of places for you once you're running on all eight cylinders. Just let me know, buddy."

He clapped my shoulder. I held the wince in, smiling, then assuring him that I would reach out once I had my life in order.

"Excuse me," I said to Nick, easing myself up and out of the chair, my crutches in hand. Phillippe glanced my way, the senator and he still chatting. "I'm fine. Just need to use the men's room."

"Okay." After my brother gave me a nod, he returned to plotting out my future. Little did he know that my future was unplottable. How could it be when I didn't even know who I was anymore? I made my way around the tables and chairs scattered about, taking care to avoid any possible trip-and-fall scenarios. The men's room was right beside the ladies, which sat to the right of the bar. The server girl was talking with the bartender when I crutched past. She twisted around to avoid looking at me. Feeling that sting, I nudged my way through the door, making my way into a stall instead of trying to use the urinals. Juggling on crutches while fishing out, then holding, my dick was just too much for me right now. Maybe later I'd be able to piss standing up again. For now, it was seated. Angling into the stall was a labor in and of itself, but I managed. Leaning my ass to the door once it was closed, I pulled in several deep breaths while sliding my phone free from the interior pocket of my jacket.

I scrolled to Cooper's office phone number—the one

his PA had said would be a direct line to her. My bladder was fine. I'd just needed some space from all the well-wishers and awkward looks. The call connected, and Brianna gave a crisp hello, which was the last thing I expected.

"I didn't expect anyone to answer," I mumbled. "It's late."

"It's transferred to my emergency cell," she explained with a chuckle.

"Oh, okay. It's Moral. It's umm... Moral Dunkirk."

"Good evening, Mr. Dunkirk. Can I help you?"

"I left, and I wanted to... can I speak to Dr. Cooper, please?"

"Of course, one moment."

I was patched through with expediency. As soon as I heard his voice, my anxiety levels dropped.

"Tell me another joke," I said in lieu of hello.

"I'm not sure that's really appropriate. Brianna seemed to think—"

"I think it's really appropriate. Tell me another joke, okay?"

There was a long pause. "What was the one-legged man doing at the ATM?"

"I don't know. What *was* the one-legged man doing at the ATM?"

"Checking his balance."

I snorted so loudly it vibrated off the cool white metal walls. "That's a good one. I want to talk to you about your ideas for me. I don't want to be a lab rat."

"I promise you that you will *not* be a lab rat."

"I've had enough poking and prodding for a long time.

I just want to find myself again. Find a new me. Find some hope. And I want you to tell me jokes. No one jokes with me anymore."

"I'll do what I can, but Brianna will wash my mouth out with soap if she hears me telling some off-color thing."

"It will be our secret then. Can you meet up with me tonight?"

"In public?!"

"No, no." I'd had enough of people gaping, gasping, and hiding their eyes. "I'll come to your tower. Is it too late to visit now?"

"Yes, I'm in my pajamas. Tomorrow morning meet me in my office. I'll give you the tour, and we'll talk in depth about what I foresee for you and me."

Someone entered the bathroom. "Moral, are you okay in here?"

My brother. I rolled my eyes. "I'm fine," I called back in French. "Give me a moment or two. Can't a man take a shit in private?"

He left in a hurry. I placed the phone back to my ear. "Sorry. Tomorrow morning is good. Nine a.m. At Stark Tower or at my place?" That made him snicker. That little laugh made me feel better.

"At Stark Tower," he confirmed

"Perfect. I just must ask. If you are Tony Stark, does that make me War Machine? There are some striking similarities."

"You're not Black."

"No, but I *did* fall from the sky and suffered permanent damage."

"Hmm, okay, I see the point you're making."

"Also, you're just as smart, and far cuter, than Tony Stark, so there is that."

There was stunned silence on the other end. It dragged on so long I began to think I'd lost service when a little cough took place.

"Let's hope that I'm as clever as Tony Stark," he whispered.

"I hope so."

There was that word again. Hope. For some crazy reason, I now had a little.

"Tomorrow at nine." A brief pause. Then in a massive rush. "You're cuter than War Machine."

The line went dead. A silly sort of grin broke free despite my best efforts. What was it about that adorable inventor that was making my spirits lift for the first time since I plummeted to Earth like Icarus? I didn't know, but I wanted more.

FIVE

Cooper
———————

HE'D CALLED ME CUTE, AND THAT HAD NEVER HAPPENED before, which made my sleep weird.

Also, for some insane reason—probably due to nerves about Moral visiting this morning—I tried a different angle for the basketball shots today, netting only seven out of ten, and having to make notes in my journal about what went wrong. Ten out of ten was perfectly possible from any decent angle, but for some reason my calculations were off today, again, probably Moral's fault, and that was a big enough blip that it needed recording. I sketched in a couple of potential arcs, added some ladybugs for bullet points, and made sure to check today's date for anything important. Of course, there'd been no chance for Brianna to add in this morning's meeting because she had no idea he was even coming. I inked in the details, and then thought I should really tell someone down at the front desk, or Brianna, or probably Tony because if my PA or my bodyguard found out I'd arranged something without any input from either one of them, they'd probably implode.

Actually, there was *no* probably about it, and I connected to him and Brianna at the same time.

"Morning. Just to let you know that Mr. Dunkirk is arriving for a nine a.m. meeting," I announced after the usual hellos. That was all I needed to say, but something was bubbling inside me, and I couldn't keep my thoughts straight. It seemed as if it was something like excitement, or maybe it was nerves. Working with Moral meant a whole new direction for how I worked. I was nervous, and yes, excited, but also scared. I wasn't sure how this was all going to work, what with me and him being in the same environment, and me not really liking the whole working with people thing. "He wants me to tell him jokes, but you know what happens when I start working? How am I supposed to tell jokes to him when I'm working out formulas?" I sat back in my chair, waiting for the advice to flow. If it wasn't Brianna with a wise tale from her youth, it was Tony telling me to 'suck it up and use my soldier spirit,' whatever that was.

"I've done all the requisite background checks," Tony said. "I'll escort him up."

Brianna joined in. "Moral signed the NDA at our last meeting." Brianna added, "Is he bringing his brother with him?"

I know she was asking me, but before I could say that I didn't know, Tony was back in with his serious vibe. "The brother's background checks are done, but not for full clearance on your floor."

"Do you have concerns?" Brianna asked.

"Not at this time," Tony replied, and through all of that, neither of them had helped me with my joke problem.

Brianna clearly had a list of things she needed to work through. "Just let me know what I need to—"

"I have a joke!" I interrupted, and we were all silent for a moment.

"I'm listening," Brianna reassured.

"Listening," Tony said at the same time.

"I want to stay professional, so you'll let me know if—"

"We'll let you know," Brianna said.

"Okay, so one-legged jokes didn't offend him, and from that, I extrapolated that he's open-minded. So how about the one with the dog and the banana?" I paused for uproar, but when both stayed silent, I forged ahead. "So, what did the dog say when he was fucking the—"

"No!" Brianna interrupted, while Tony simply snorted a laugh. "Stay away from those jokes for now, Cooper, okay? I know Mr. Dunkirk's probably heard worse on the ice, but he's here to work with you on a professional basis."

Right. I'd never had the compulsion to work with anyone, but life was a learning process, and I could handle this. I needed to keep this thing with the sexy, intriguing Moral on a strictly professional level. It can't be hard to do that. I've been avoiding connections all my life, so wanting to connect with Moral meant I was either coming down with something, or Moral was just too damn hot for me to stay focused. "Okay. Got it. No swearing."

"No, I didn't mean that, just that sexual—"

"No, it's okay. I've made a note in my journal. I'll find some more one-legged jokes instead."

Brianna let out a squeak, but we'd finished with the call. I was eager to get organized for when Moral arrived, which according to my watch was ten minutes, so I made a few polite noises and, then, hung up. I never could understand why people stayed on the phone so long, talking about this and that, when it was way more efficient to put questions in an email.

With exactly nine minutes to go, I opened my journal again and made some notes in the margin of today's page. It was important that I covered the steps of the journey we were undertaking. Since I wasn't an expert on the physical side of prosthetics, just knowing things like tensile strength and experiment results didn't help me when it came to the medical side and the actual fitting of a prosthetic. I added notes about medical implications, which carried over to the next page, and sent a quick message to Brianna about getting our newly hired prosthetics expert, Dr. Alice Kelly, up here at ten. I wanted an hour with Moral to test the water and find out what he needed from me, and what I expected from him.

When nine a.m. came and went and the hand moved toward three minutes past, I couldn't help worrying, which turned to agitation, which morphed into being cross. I wanted to move things along, not waste time staring at the elevator, all while wishing the light would indicate Moral was on his way up.

By nine-thirteen, confusion consumed me because this is what happens to me. I open up to help someone, give them the benefit of all the science they could want, but they leave me alone, as if I don't deserve their time or respect. He said he'd be here at nine, but nine-fourteen on my incredibly accurate watch mocked me.

Finally, the light flickered, and the doors opened soon after. Moral and Tony spilled out into the lobby on the twenty-fifth floor, and I was deep into defense mode, which must have shown in my expression because Tony stopped dead.

"Sorry I'm late." Moral was breathing heavily. "The cab couldn't stop outside the building, and I had to climb stairs when I was accosted by your private army."

"I don't have an army." I turned to Tony. "Do I?"

"No, you don't have an army," Tony reassured me.

"But someone accosted you?" That seemed like an old-fashioned word, but the way Moral said it, with the softness of his accent, made it seem like this sensual wisp of something that I wanted to grab hold of.

It's inappropriate to think about how sexy Moral's voice is.

"Ray didn't accost your guest, he just wanted to see ID," Tony defended to me.

Moral threw my bodyguard a grumpy scowl, which didn't bode well for how today's meeting was going to go. "Did you miss the bit where I had to climb six sets of stairs?"

"I apologize—" I began.

"Your security should know how to handle... this..." He nodded his head to indicate his leg, and I realized we were all just standing there like idiots. My ire at Moral being late had dissipated as soon as I took in his pale skin and pinched expression. Clearly, my inconvenience of thirteen minutes or so was nothing to what he'd had to go through to get here.

"I'll ask Brianna to arrange the appropriate training," Tony said, then stepped back in the elevator.

"Damn it to hell, fucking useless leg," Moral said in snapped French.

Now what?

Moral leaned heavily on his crutches, white knuckling them. The last thing he needed was to be hanging around the floor lobby. I should offer him a drink and somewhere to rest up.

"Would you like a drink?"

"Whiskey neat," he murmured and shifted his balance, wincing as he moved.

"Are you on medication? That isn't really what—"

"Water is fine, brains. I was being sarcastic."

Brains? Like I hadn't heard that joke before. I could read his expression, understood his sarcasm, but maybe I should make a joke now. Only he winced again, and I needed to get him seated, and hydrated, and then we could start our chat.

I led him through to the sofas, which Brianna had installed in case I had meetings up here. Spoiler alert: I didn't do meetings in my space, at least not until the board's instructions meant I had to. At least I was having a meeting with someone I liked, so there was that.

"Do you need some painkillers?" I asked as I handed him the glass. He unfurled his hand, and I identified a couple of the pills in his palm, but others, I had no idea about.

"Already on it."

I perched on the sofa opposite him as he swallowed the meds. Now was as good a time as any to set initial boundaries. "It's important that you are honest with me about medication, and addiction, so I can assess the significance of—"

"I don't have addictions," he growled at me, his hazel eyes sparking, and I wondered if he had a fiery temper to match his hair.

"Oh, I wasn't suggesting that—"

"I was once checked so hard it loosened a tooth, and you know what I did? I pulled it out and kept on playing. Didn't need meds or help, and I didn't need either when I cracked ribs in the next game, or when I fractured my jaw at the end of last season. I take what the docs tell me, but only if I really have to, so if you think for one minute I'm addicted to anything, you're wrong."

I observed him getting more and more irritated, and finally held up a hand to stop him.

"So, you're stubborn."

He blinked at me, his mouth dropping open in surprise. "The fuck—"

I interrupted him and forged ahead. "And you're wrong, because *everyone* has addictions, or at least things that are a fixed part of their life."

He sipped his water, then carefully placed it on the table next to him. I don't know what half the meds were that he'd swallowed, but the tension bracketing his mouth seemed to lessen with each passing moment. Never could I imagine the broken bones and pain, or the sheer horror of what had happened to him, and a lesser man may not even have made it to this point. I'd seen the photos of the plane,

I'd had a doctor talk me through all the words used in Moral's medical report, and I knew he'd been so close to dying that there must have been moments where he wanted to never come back.

"Hockey," he said simply. "I've lived and breathed hockey since I was tiny, and it's everything to me." He clenched his hands into fists in his lap. "And it doesn't matter what you do, or what I've been talked into doing, hockey is gone." He loosened one fist and rubbed above his knee, and I wondered if maybe phantom hurt was pushing through the soft cloud of pain meds.

"You should find something else that you can be addicted to," I announced, as if that would fix it all. "Do you game? I mean video games, that kind of thing."

"Xavier tried to get me into D&D a while back. He's a close friend and teammate, so I gave it a chance, but somehow I always died."

A twinge of jealousy snapped in my chest at the thought of some other man being Moral's close friend. And yes, I knew I was being irrational, and I lacked experience with having *weird feelings* where Moral was concerned. Or something. I had researched the fascination I had with the big man, and my dick certainly seemed interested in what I'd found when my research took me to porn that included a big bear of a man and an itty-bitty small guy. Not that I fit in the undersized range when I checked average height charts. I was still five-ten, and maybe a little on the too-slim side in the whole weight area, but next to him being a sequoia, I was just a sapling.

"Are you listening?" he asked with a hint of impatience.

"Yes, of course," I lied.

"Sex with aliens," he said, and now it was my turn to blink at him.

"Huh?"

"See, you weren't listening!"

"I was, I mean, maybe I was thinking complicated math at that very moment."

He raised a single red eyebrow, and then rolled his eyes in the exact way that Tony did whenever I did anything stupid.

He cleared his throat. "I said good luck with finding something better than hockey. I loved swimming, skydiving, horseback riding, driving. I mean, I have a garage full of these amazing cars I can't even drive anymore. Did you know I have a 1956 Ferrari 290 MM?"

"That's a car, right? Not an electric one, obviously. And no; it wasn't in the information pack that Tony and Brianna made up for me."

This time, he smiled. "She's stunning."

"And probably fully adaptable."

He gasped, "You can't adapt a Ferrari 290."

"Okay, then swimming."

"Yep, can't do that anymore," he said it as if it was a done deal.

"You can."

"Nope, I just flip over, no balance, and I can't get the rhythm."

"So, you gave up?" I knew that was a dangerous thing to ask a person who appeared to have spent their whole life confronting danger, but I wanted to know his thought process.

"I didn't give up."

"You just said you *don't* swim anymore."

"I can't exactly knock out a hundred lengths, can I? And people watch and point, even in rehab, and I don't want to be the center of some kind of freak show."

Oh, and there it was. He felt like he couldn't perform as well as he'd used to, and he didn't want to be watched. That was a vital clue that maybe wasn't in the info pack. I felt quite clever at this point, as if I'd solved the Goldbach conjecture and shown the world just how easy life could be with the answers. Then inspiration hit me.

"Come with me," I said, pressing the intercom and connecting to Tony. "Tony, can you extend Moral's security to my floor? We're going swimming."

Behind me, Moral was disagreeing. "We're not—"

I waved a hand at him. "Also, can you ask Brianna to organize lunch for when Dr. Kelly is here?"

"Okay, although you're taking our visitor to the top floor, are you sure?"

I remember clearly saying that there was no way a stranger would be allowed up in my space. Of course, I hadn't met Moral then, and something in me wanted to give him the chance to discover that he could still enjoy swimming. "Yeah, I changed my mind."

There was the longest pause, and I imagined Tony digesting the news. "I'm on it."

When I ended the call, Moral was still blustering in his native tongue about swimming and not having trunks and his leg. I definitely heard him curse me and call me a fucking idiot at least twice. Probably better to let him know I speak his language before this went much further.

"Nous allons nager," I announced. *We're going swimming.*

"Wait, you speak French?" he asked with shock.

"I do."

He muttered again, then threw his hands in the air. "Well, that's just fucking awesome. But just for the record, your accent is for shit." He folded his arms over his chest as if he wanted to start a fight that might delay going upstairs.

"It's perfectly acceptable," I defended. "We're not fighting about it, and we're still going swimming."

SIX

Moral
_____

THIS MORNING HAD BEEN ONE OF DISCOVERY.

For starters, this tower needed more handicapped accessibility. I suspected Cooper would be on that yesterday. He seemed the type to not let things sit unattended.

Second, the good doctor of... well, whatever he was a doctor of... inevitability? I didn't know, but the good doctor spoke French. With a horrid accent, but he spoke it fluently.

Third, for such a small and scholarly man, Cooper was stubborn as a moose. And moose can be quite bullheaded.

Ha. Bullheaded. A moose. Ah, see, Dunny is buried in there somewhere, Moral.

I coughed up a laugh as I sat in a changing room just off the massive indoor pool, staring down at the swim trunks Tony—who I suspected was an ex-Treadstone operative à la Jason Bourne—had handed to me. I'd been here less than an hour, and they had trunks for me. In my size and preferred color of blue. How did they know I liked blue? Had I mentioned it in conversation? Online? Maybe.

I said lots of silly things on my social media accounts. Or I used to. Now, I never posted anything. Glancing down at my stump, I sighed. Who wanted to see that? I could barely stand to look at or touch it. There was nothing gross about it now. The flesh had healed perfectly. It was smooth, pink, and according to my surgeon ready for a permanent prosthesis. The temporary one had not suited me well. I'd worn it during my therapy back home, but it was ill-fitting and uncomfortable. Heavy, cumbersome, ugly, fake. I'd hated it, and tossed it aside after each round of PT, going back to crutches, which had their own issues. The wheelchair was only for extreme situations. I loathed being wheeled around like an invalid.

"Mr. Dunkirk? Are you okay in there?"

I jumped at the soft rap on the dressing room door.

"I'm fine, Tony."

"Very well, sir. Shout if you need assistance. I'm right outside the door."

Great. The CIA assassin was keeping tabs on me. What exactly did he think I was going to do? Roll after his boss? Waffle the doctor with my crutch? And then what? To what end? Industrial espionage was kind of out of my league. I was a hockey player with a degree in art history. Also, I was kind of lumbering and awkward at the moment.

Moral, stop. The guy is not black ops.

Are we sure?

No. But you're using this to postpone sliding on those trunks. You can do this.

What will Cooper think when he sees my leg?

My inner voice had no reply to that. I reached down to rub the scar. Part of my new daily routine was desensitization and scar massage. Phillippe had done it for me several times early on, but even his hands on the neatly healed stub made me cringe. Four times a day—if I remembered. I would run a spiky massage ball over the stump for several minutes, then I would massage near the scar. This was all supposed to help in making the scar less sensitive and aid in the prosthesis process. And it had worked. At first, I could barely stand a soft towel being rubbed over the surgery site. Now, I was up to spiky massage balls, which was probably all that would ever touch it. What man or woman would wish to caress such a thing? Or hear the melancholy ramblings of a has-been-someone facing an uphill journey behind a motherfucking massive boulder. Me and Sisyphus. I suspected that I'd be bowled over by the rock more than once as I tried to reach the summit.

After giving the area a nervous rubdown, I wiggled to the end of the chair, eased my boxers down, and pulled on the trunks. Then I sat back, pushed up with my good leg, and eased them under and over my ass. Okay. Good. Now, I just had to get my backside up and head to the pool. Yep. Here we go then.

Five minutes passed. I ran a finger over each new scar on my body. So many of them, bright pink against my skin, the one on my shoulder surrounded by freckles from my time shirtless out in the sun. God but I missed the outdoors.

Then stop moping and get up! This man can get you back outside.

My head was a muddle. One part of me wanted to get back to doing all I had before the crash. The other half wanted to hide in this little cabana room and never leave. The continual back-and-forth was mentally exhausting. Why could I not stop being so weak and indecisive?!

"Moral," Cooper called through the door. I pulled my sight from my leg to stare at the door. "Are you in need of help?"

"I want things to be the way they used to be," I replied, unsure of why I was even saying that to someone I had just met. He wasn't my mental health counselor or physical therapist or even a surgeon. Why the hell was I laying that on his doorstep?

"That will never happen," he answered, turning the knob slowly, then easing his head through. His hair was a terrible mess, which seemed to be his everyday appearance.

"You're not supposed to say that. You're supposed to blow smoke up my ass like my brother and everyone else. And you're supposed to tell me that if I just work hard, everything will be just as it had been."

"Well, that's not entirely true." He picked up my crutches and handed them to me. "You can certainly live a full and rewarding life after losing a limb, but things will never be the same. You'll never play for the Rebels again, but with some help from me and a lot of sweat, you could skate again. Again, that will never happen if you don't get in that pool. Oh. That's a lovely looking stump. The healing rate is quite good. I've been reading up. May I examine it more closely?"

"No." His gaze flew from my leg to my shocked face.

He blushed hot pink. It was a good look. "I am sorry. That was incredibly rude. I tend to get… well, I tend to get lost in the science of things. I should not have asked to examine your leg. That would be like asking someone if you could check out their penis."

"I'd mind that a lot less to be frank. I have a great cock. Very pretty, so I'm told. That stump is… it is not pretty at all."

Cooper cleared his throat. "I think it's a fine stump. The surgeon did an excellent job. And it's healed nicely. I cannot comment on your cock. Although, I *would* be interested in knowing if your libido is in any way suffering since the loss of your limb. Are you experiencing sexual urges now that the pain has lessened? What do you think the emotional trauma has done to your erection rates per day? Have you seen a marked increase in nocturnal emissions?"

Tony coughed so loudly on the other side of the door that I feared he might be hacking up a lung. I simply stared for the longest time as Cooper blushed to the tips of his ears. Then I laughed. Hard and long.

"You are cute," I gasped when the giggle fit ended. "Thank you for being so… you. It's refreshing to not have people force-feeding me positivity *all day long*. Sometimes I need to be quiet and down, yes?"

"Yes, we all need to have balance. Are you ginger all over?"

"Okay, boss, we better get into the pool," Tony interrupted him, thus cutting off my reply neatly, which was probably for the best, as I was going to offer to show Cooper if the curtains matched the drapes. "Brianna wanted me to remind you that you have a meeting with the development team from NASA for that miniaturization project, as well as Dr. Kelly's visit."

Cooper nodded. "Right. NASA. I'd much rather be in the pool. I find the water really soothing. At one time, I hypothesized that people who loved the water were direct descendants of Atlantis. What do you think?"

"I, umm… seems reasonable," I replied as we made our way to this pool. The air was thick with the smell of chlorine. One wall was thick glass that looked down over Boston, the others cool blue tiles.

"Be careful here, the tiles are wet and can be slippery," Cooper warned, sliding an arm around me as if he would be able to stop my burly ass if I went down. The skim of his fingers across my bare back sent a soft buzzing heat to my balls. My dick woke from its months' long nap. Huh. That was nice. I'd been wondering if I'd ever pop a boner again. Of course, this was not the appropriate place, but even a half chub was cause for jubilation. "Now we're just going to ease you into the water from a sitting position in the shallow end. I have workmen coming to install a chairlift."

"That's not necessary," I argued, but he didn't seem to hear me.

"Also, I want to devote some of our time into crafting a shower and swim leg for you. You do like to spend time on the water, correct? I did see that in your files. Fishing, canoeing, kayaking. That sort of woodsy stuff."

"That would be cool." I eyed the water warily. My first few times in a pool after the surgery had not gone well. Tony appeared on my left, took my crutches, then eased my weight onto his wide shoulders. Together, we lowered my ass onto the side of the pool. Using my arms, I carefully moved myself down the stairs, one at a time, until the warm water was lapping at my collarbones. I drew in a long breath, let it out, and tried to focus on Cooper. He walked down the stairs, clad in his trunks and a T-shirt that read "Sheldon Cooper's Fun with Flags" on the front.

"I like the shirt," I commented.

"Oh," he glanced down at his chest, "people think it's funny that we share the same name. I'm not sure it's funny, but the material is soft."

"Cool." I didn't know what else to say.

He sat down beside me, gaze never leaving my face, and removed a red pair of glasses, then handed them to Tony. "Are you comfortable so far?"

"Yeah, it's okay." And it was.

"Good. Tony, can you fetch the unicorns?" He sat primly at my side, his tee sticking to his lean form nicely.

I craned my head to watch his bodyguard walk to one of several doors around the pool, open it, enter, and come out a second later with inflatable rainbow unicorns. I chuckled at the sight. Tony seemed less than impressed, but he never said a word, just tossed the two blow up toys into the water in front of us.

"Excellent! Now, let's get you swimming." He grabbed one unicorn, pulled it around his thin waist, and then began paddling away from the stairs. I did the same, the fit a little snug for me, but I eased away from the safety of the steps. The floatation device kept me from flipping over or sinking, as I'd done previously.

"Do I look stupid?" I shouted as I worked to catch up with Cooper.

"You look magnificent!" he called back over his shoulder. It felt odd as hell. There was no resistance on the one side, and that kept slowing me down, frustrating me. "We're not racing," he said, paddling back to me. "We're just working on getting you used to the imbalance that you'll face in the water. Once you adjust, we'll move onto different strokes and build on your balance as you enter and leave the pool. One day, you'll be able to balance on your one leg and dive into the water."

"That would be... very nice. Yes, very nice indeed." And so I paddled around the pool like a toddler, with an inflatable unicorn around my waist, listening to Cooper prattling on about any number of things. Most science-related, as that seemed to be his happy place. Science and this pool. He did seem to enjoy the water. Maybe he *did* have the blood of Atlanteans.

"Can I ask you something?" I enquired when we ended our hour. It went so quickly I didn't even notice the time flying past. We were sitting on the edge of the pool, our three feet dangling in the water, towels around our shoulders.

"Of course. The only way to learn is to question." He

splashed his feet like a child, a smile on his face that was adorable beyond words.

"Why do you wear a T-shirt in the pool?"

The splashing stopped. He threw a look my way, his hair sticking to his skull, his glasses back on his nose, but covered with water droplets from his incessant kicking. His shoulders rose, his mouth pulled down. "If that makes you uncomfortable, then you don't have to answer."

"No, it's only fair that, if I ask for frank and honest replies from you, I give you the same in return." He pushed up his glasses with a water-wrinkled finger. "I feel inadequate about my physique, especially around sexy, manly men like you."

He thought I was sexy. Wow! That was... unexpected. How could he find me sexy after eyeballing what was left of my leg?

"You have a nice body. It's compact, tight, and wiry. I like it a lot," I earnestly replied. He glanced my way with a shy little sideways peek that made my belly feel fuzzy. "I bet you'd fit right on my lap for a good cuddle."

He stared at me through his water-speckled glasses, then a tiny smile tugged at the corners of his mouth.

"I don't much like cuddles," he whispered. "But I'd like to try... one day." All sorts of things began happening in my swim trunks. I was about to reach over for him, lift him up and settle him on my thighs, when Tony's watch alarm went off, filling the huge room with a shrill beeping noise.

"That's Brianna. NASA is waiting for you downstairs," Tony informed Cooper, who sighed heavily, then slowly got to his feet. "Then you have a meeting with Dr. Kelly."

"I have to go. Tony will assist you to the showers and with getting dressed if you require any help. Then, he'll escort you to my place, get you a bite of something that you enjoy, and by then Dr. Kelly and I should be back for your consultation. Make sure to let Tony know what you'd like to nibble on to tide you over until we have lunch with Dr. Kelly."

You. I'd like Tony to bring me you to nibble on.

I bit back that comment, nodded, smiled, and watched Cooper pad off with slappy, wet feet to the door we had entered through.

"Hey!" I shouted. Cooper stopped and turned to face me. I twisted around on the wet tiles to look at him. "You didn't tell me a joke today."

Cooper smiled widely. "I dated a one-legged guy who worked in a beer factory. He was in charge of hops."

That one made me roar. I was still chuckling when Tony hoisted me to my foot and passed me my crutches.

"Your boss is funny," I told the man strolling along at my side, presumably to keep me from having a slip-and-fall accident. "Is he seeing anyone?" I asked as nonchalantly as possible.

"He's quite the punster. As for dating... umm, no, not right now. He's not much for interpersonal relations, to be honest. The fact that he allowed you into his inner sanctum has all of us scratching our heads."

"Must be he has a thing for gimpy gingers," I commented, easing into the dressing room all by myself—thank you—and sitting down with a huff. "So he doesn't invite men or women into his place often?"

"Never. He never invites *anyone* to his private floors.

I'll be right outside if you need anything." With that, he closed the door to let me change and ruminate on exactly what the heck was brewing with me and Cooper. Whatever it was, I'd not felt this light and hopeful in forever. I prayed that the feeling would last. I rather liked the sun being in my life again.

SEVEN

Cooper

_____

NASA MADE ME ANTSY AND ANGRY AND IRRATIONAL.

They didn't mean to, but they weren't listening, and I really wanted to get back up to Moral and have lunch and talk to Dr. Kelly about prosthetics. And now the miniaturization project that NASA wanted me to work on was just boring.

"… about the other way you might shrink a human? Could we take away atoms proportionately from every part of the person we're trying to shrink?" The NASA guy leading this team was very earnest, and normally, that was a question I'd love to debate at length. But today, all I wanted to do was leave.

"Most living things are the size they are because that is the size that works for how they are built," I offered, and the NASA guy in charge blinked at me. "For example, what does adenosine tri-phosphate do when one of the phosphorus atoms is removed? Or if one or two oxygen atoms are removed from each phosphate group? Does your atom-removing shrinking machine care which kind of bond the oxygen atom had to the phosphorus? The test subject's nerves would no longer work and photochemical reactions in their eyes would cease, but being blind would be the least of your worries as their vagus nerve would stop regulating."

"Doctor—"

"I really need to go. Perhaps we could pick that up another day? More research is needed and I…" Glancing helplessly at Tony, I saw he went from surprised, to dead-ass special ops guy in an instant. He blocked me from the others in the room and hurried me out. I sent Brianna a wince of apology as I passed her but didn't stop to talk as she moved in to placate the team who'd already waited three months for an appointment. I love what NASA wanted to do in terms of space exploration, but I wasn't Elon Musk, and I didn't want to break the Earth's boundaries in the same way as he did—my feet were firmly on the ground in bettering the planet we had now by accidentally discovering new things. But one line in a recent interview about the old Dennis Quade movie *Inner Space*, and NASA was all over me. I just loved eighties movies, particularly science fiction with all the things they got wrong. I never expected anyone to actually take from a throwaway comment that I wanted to work on miniaturizing anything.

I could feel Tony's questioning gaze on me as we waited for the elevator, and I stared ahead stoically, hoping he didn't voice a single one of them in case I had to answer.

"So, you let him up to your floor," he said, and there went any chance of me not explaining myself.

"He said he couldn't swim anymore," I said.

"You never let anyone up to that floor," Tony challenged me.

I side-eyed him, ready to ignore that comment, but immediately wilted under his penetrating stare. I didn't know much about Tony's backstory—Brianna and Uncle Jeremiah were the ones who'd hired him—but I bet he could make even the strongest person break just by staring at them.

"He can't hurt me," I defended.

"Neither could that scrawny intern you had last summer that you bonded with, but you never let *him* upstairs."

Well, that was true, but then Alfie, despite our shared love of science, had been another tech-head like me and not someone built by nature to be big and brawny and red-haired and sexy. I didn't want people in my space. They made messes and asked awkward questions and took me out of my routine, but... Moral wasn't people.

He was...

... something else.

I just hadn't figured out what yet, but his comment about having me on his knee for a cuddle was enough to have me blushing even now. Normally the thought of doing that would horrify me, but a small part of me wanted to sit on Moral's knee and cling to him like a limpet, and then lean in and—

"Are you okay?" Tony pressed a hand to my forehead,

and I stepped back to avoid him fussing. "You're bright red."

"I'm fine." I noticed the elevator stopped on twenty-one, and I rolled my eyes. "I need a dedicated elevator," I announced because that was a sore point for Tony, and it would change the subject.

"And again, no you don't because a: it's a security risk having you in a specific target and b: you never go anywhere often enough to warrant it."

"But what if me using random elevators means I put everyone else in them at risk?"

Tony raised an eyebrow, and I shrugged as the elevator finally arrived at the third floor where the NASA meeting had been, and we were standing, waiting for it. The doors opened, and Tony went in first, his eyes checking each corner. I followed him when he nodded and scanned a card against the panel on the wall. Now the elevator would head to the penthouse without stopping.

"What if NASA actually does manage to miniaturize humans and a teeny-tiny hitman gets in through an air filter?"

Tony's eyebrow climbed even higher. "Then the teeny tiny human would feel the weight of my not so teeny-tiny fist and splat!" He made a splat motion with his hand, and I immediately felt sorry for the improbable assassin who wouldn't last a second with Tony, although I spotted a fault in his reasoning.

"How would you spot them in the first place?"

"With my teeny-tiny-assassin scanner," he deadpanned, as the elevator reached the top and stopped.

"You have one of those?" I asked.

"Nope, but the minute NASA can shrink humans, I'd need you to invent one for me," he responded, which made absolute sense in my head.

"Okay, got it. If NASA shrinks humans, then I'll invent a scanner to be able to squash miniature assassins. Get Brianna to add it to my to-do list."

I was still smiling when we went into the huge kitchen in my apartment space, but it fell when I saw a few things at the same time.

A dark-haired woman in a suit was sitting on a stool at the counter nursing a coffee and looking as if she needed a hug. I assumed it was Dr. Kelly.

And there was Moral, standing at a far window in the living room, staring into the middle distance, leaning on crutches, and looking as if maybe he'd been the one to cause the woman to need a hug. His expression was bleak, and that didn't bode well for anything at all.

"Dr. Kelly?" I asked, and she stood up and extended her hand, which I shook because I assumed she'd been vetted and checked to within an inch of her life.

"Call me Evelyn, Dr. Harvey," she replied.

"Cooper, and uh, what happened?" I waved in the general direction of Moral, who hadn't moved. I wondered if he even knew I was in the room, or whether he was ignoring me and Tony.

"Entirely my fault," Evelyn said, and her shoulders hunched. "I'm a huge Rebels fan. I don't know what I was thinking. We were talking, and he seemed fine, but then I started talking about Lomac, and he went all broody. I get why it happened, and it's not like me to fuck up, but I did."

I couldn't work out what she meant by Lomac, and

Tony had disappeared to do whatever ninja-bodyguards did. "What does Lomac stand for?"

"Stand for?" She seemed confused and then lowered her voice. "Oh sorry, no. Lomac is a person, Logan Mackie. They've just announced he's being pulled up from the Schooners. The Essex Schooners. The AHL team? He's a rental, y'know, moves around and fills empty spots for a year, then has to move on."

Clearly, my research hadn't gone that far, and I shrugged.

"Oh well, Logan is Moral's replacement, in a way. I mean, they shuffled the lines, pushed Austin Rowe to the second line, but mostly Logan Mackie is—"

Holding up a hand to stop her, I replied, "I'll talk to Moral," then left before Evelyn-the-doc could bamboozle me with more hockey. I knew what lines were—hell, I knew the mechanics of the game, and the rules—but I hadn't dug deep into personnel. I knew who Austin Rowe was from my research—some bright new star who was part of a family dynasty or something—but I certainly didn't know this Logan Mackie guy. Still, I didn't have to be a genius to understand that Moral being *replaced* had to hurt in ways I could never understand. And that was on top of the swimming and me pushing and everything else.

Some people said I lacked empathy. I mean, I'd heard it a million times, but what they never understood was that it was me lacking patience with their issues. Too much to do and too little time.

But Moral?

I wanted to take time to go over and listen and understand, but most of all, I wanted to make him smile --

that was a brand-new feeling for me. I wished I had an inner jock that I could channel, but I didn't have that in any sense of the word, so as I walked over to him, I had to just be me.

For what it was worth.

"Hey." Never let it be said I wasn't the master of conversation.

He seemed to come out of some trance-like state, slowly turning his head to look at me and blinking as if he'd stepped into the light from a dark room.

"Hey," he murmured, and I realized I was lost in his hazel eyes, imagining I could see pain there.

"You want to come and talk? Get something to eat."

He glanced over his shoulder, wobbling on his crutches a little. I immediately went to steady him and gripped his shirt sleeve. He turned back, looked down at my hand, and then back up to my face.

"You can let go," he murmured. It sounded more like a demand than a suggestion, so I did. "I owe Dr. Kelly an apology," he added, and slowly turned on his crutches, wincing as he did. I can't imagine what it was like to heave the bulk of himself using the crutches under his arms—the pressure and bruising, and the aches in muscles must be intense.

"I need to invent crutches that don't hurt, maybe with suspension or from a lighter material," I mused and followed him back to the kitchen to where Dr. Kelly sat waiting. He never said a word back to me, simply shuffled himself to the stool opposite the doc and offered a smile to her.

"Sorry about that—"

"I'm so sorry—"

They talked over each other and ended up nodding with mutual respect. I guess that was done then.

When Tony was back -- from one of his perimeter checks, I assumed -- he watched in silence as the three of us ate the offered snacks and sandwiches and talked about the medical side of what we were trying to do.

By the time Dr. Kelly left, close to five p.m., Moral was looking pale and exhausted, and my brain hurt with all the extra information I needed to add into the equation that was helping amputees. Or more specifically, helping Moral.

"I need to call a cab," he murmured as he slumped back on the sofa and listed sideways.

"Tony will take you home," I said immediately and checked with Tony, who was sitting on a kitchen stool eating leftover snacks. He nodded his assent, but when I turned back to Moral his eyes were closed and his breathing even. He'd fallen asleep on the sofa, and I changed my mind. "Can you help me make him comfortable?" I asked Tony, who readily helped. Between the two of us, we put cushions in place, moved him carefully so he was comfortable, and covered him with a blanket.

"I think I'm done for the day," I told Tony, who only hesitated for the shortest time, then nodded, did some final checks, and left for his place on the floor below. Though I know he had a team on me at all times -- and probably a life outside of looking out for me -- I never got a hint of it, nor had any need to know about it before tonight. I don't know what it was, but something compelled me to comment as we parted at the elevator.

"I need to tell Brianna that we should move on with the apartment for Moral."

"The team is vetted and has all supplies ready to go... they just need your okay."

"Oh, okay then. Go for it."

"Mr. Dunkirk is definitely going to be staying here and working with you?"

"Why? Did he say otherwise? Does he hate being here? Have I messed up? Does he hate me?"

Tony frowned. "Not at all. I was just checking with you before we disrupt your work."

"Oh, okay." Now I was embarrassed and cursed that I let my insecurities show, so I rapidly changed the subject. "Do you have anything planned for tonight?" I asked, and he was instantly confused. Not only had I followed him to the elevator, but I'd asked him questions. Even I didn't know what was going on, so I bet it was a shock to him.

"Dinner with my brother and sister-in-law, but they're coming here, so I'm available if you need me."

"That wasn't why I was asking, I just wanted to know..." if he had a life outside of always being with me.

"If I what?"

The ding of the arriving elevator startled us both. "Do I take up too much of your time?"

"It's my job," he explained, but very cautiously.

"But I take up a lot of your time, and I worry that you're lonely?" Oh, for God's sake, now I was channeling some great inner confusion of my own and dumping it on him. *Damn Moral with his smile and his body and his worming his way into my thoughts.*

"Lonely? Of course not. My wife balances childcare and writing."

"Your wife? Childcare?"

"Yes, you know… the family who lives in a luxurious apartment that came with my job. The one right below yours where my children have so much space that we even have an indoor adventure playground that I built a few months back."

He went into the elevator and pressed a button.

"Wait, you have children? And a wife? How did I not know this?"

"Don't ask, don't tell," Tony quipped, and the door closed between us. I made a note on my phone to ask Brianna for details and hurried back to the cozy sofa where a sleeping giant was snoring gently. After watching him for a bit, I went to grab some of the snacks Tony had put in the refrigerator, and when I returned, I sat in the chair opposite Moral and watched him sleep.

Not in a creepy way, of course. But in a concerned, wondering, calculating, experimenting in-my-head kind of way. Then, I researched what the AHL was, and who this Lomac guy was, and ended up in yet another rabbit hole of information about hockey and lines and teams and finally I hit Moral's name, losing myself in memes and twitter for a while. I needed to think about the prosthetic and the stump. Moral was asleep, so I could just…

I tugged back the blanket, exposing the stump, sketching the shape of it on my notepad, and got lost in the list of things I could invent to make things better for him.

Moral stirred just before eleven, opening his eyes and blinking up at the ceiling, looking all kinds of confused. After a few moments, he turned to look out at the room and me.

"What happened?"

"You fell asleep, and we didn't want to disturb you."

"What are you doing?" He glanced down where his stump was exposed and tugged the cover over it.

"I was sketching your injuries to work out what—"

"You were staring at me?"

"No—"

"Don't you fucking do that again, you hear me?" He attempted to sit up, cursing as he flailed. When he finally righted himself, I closed the notebook. He was scarlet with anger, and I needed to explain that I wasn't staring in a bad way, but that I was working.

"I needed to make sure—"

"I'm not an experiment. I've told you that. Staring at me when I'm asleep and laughing at what's left of me!"

"No, I wasn't—"

"I want to go home."

"It's late—"

"Call me a fucking cab or I'll do it myself!" He attempted to stand, and I did the only thing I could think of. I pressed the emergency call button for Tony.

In the chaos that followed, I had to stand back and watch. Tony was with me in under a minute, gun drawn, and only when he'd checked out everything did he get Moral ready to leave my apartment saying he'd take him home.

"Fuck you," Moral snapped, shoving Tony away,

which was no mean feat, then losing his balance and crashing back into the wall. "Don't touch me!"

"Mr. Dunkirk—"

"I'm getting a cab."

All I could do was watch the elevator doors begin to close. It was Moral who had the last pain filled words.

"I'm not coming back!"

EIGHT

Moral

TWO DAYS LATER, I WAS BACK.

It pissed me off that I gave into my sister-in-law so quickly. Yuka always knew just what buttons to push to get me to do whatever she thought was best for me. Mostly, she was right. I'd never admit that to my brother. Hell, I barely admitted it to myself. Deep down, she knew that I knew that she knew she was smarter than me for just about everything, including my life and what I needed. Someone needed to sort me out because, frankly, I was a damn mess on legs. Leg. Single.

Phillippe had made himself scarce this morning after we'd had a long sit-down from Tony-the-bodyguard about not upsetting Dr. Harvey and controlling one's temper and how this was someone's home and not a hockey rink and that I was a guest who should behave accordingly. Nothing like being made to feel like a three-year-old on top of being shamed, sickened, and generally depressed, leaving me to my own devices. Cooper was keeping his distance, the poor guy. I really felt terrible about how I'd overreacted. It had been made clear upon signing onto this field trial/clinical trial/experimental run that people other than me would be looking at and touching my stump. I mean, yeah, obviously. It was all medical. Professional. Cold. Detached. Like how every human being regarded me now. As if I were less than. A freak. Something to be pitied. I loathed the looks of pity and disgust. Women and men used to glance at me and smile in appreciation. Now they drew back. Kids stared or pointed.

Lost in a deep pit of depression and self-hate, with a generous dollop of fury at the God who I had worshipped for years, for allowing this horror to befall me. What kind of deity would make a child of his suffer so? I needed to know. I crutched around the upper floors of the tower until I found a gym. And by gym, I mean state-of-the art gymnasium that could put the Rebels facility to shame gym. Who used it? I hadn't a clue. Probably Tony. The guy was in incredible shape. Maybe Cooper walks on the treadmill while doing scientific equations in his head.

The place was all cool shades of black, gray, white, and silver. I passed the bikes and the treadmills, and plopped my sorry ass down on the seated shoulder press machine for starters. Removing my tee, I began working my upper body, reps for my shoulders to start. Then onto chest presses, adding more and more weight as I moved into the seated row, then lat pull-downs. Twenty reps each before adding more weight. Over and over I lifted, the clanking and huffing easing me into a zone that erased everything but the burn of working muscles.

When I ran out of juice, I took a breather, wiping my face with my Rebels T-shirt, sweat running down my spine. My gaze roved the room, landing on the bench press set-up. Before the crash, I could bench eighty percent of my body weight with ease. Being two hundred twenty-five pounds, that would put me at around a hundred eighty-five pounds, which I'd always gone well beyond. I could do that again. My arms were strong, reliable, still whole. For the most part. The shoulder was new, but I'd completed the PT for that and had been pronounced fit and ready for life. Life meaning getting on that fucking bench and showing the world that I was still strong. Still a man.

Hey, Dumbo, you got a spotter?

Spotter. Pfft. I don't need no stinking spotter.

Gimping my way to the bench, I added the necessary weight that I was lifting BC. Before Crash. A nice round two hundred pounds. Lying down, I stared at the ceiling, then the bar, then the ceiling. I exhaled, grabbed the bar, making sure my forearms were in a vertical line, hips firm on the bench, and lifted. It was like riding a bike. I'd been lifting weights since I was a young teenager. The bar lifted with ease. The first time. Without having two feet to plant on the ground to stabilize my body, my balance was off. I didn't notice it too badly at first, but after several reps, the pull across my shoulders and upper chest became noticeable. Still, I pushed through, realigning myself, set on getting to my BC speed of twenty-five reps per minute. After ten or so reps, I felt a twinge in my shoulder and locked my arms, the bar bowing over my chest, high in the air.

"Fuck," I wheezed through clenched teeth.

"Where's your spotter, asshole?" Someone who sounded a lot like Marquis Miller asked from behind me. He was dressed in workout gear of black Nike shorts and a white tank top, and wrapped his hands around the bar. "You're overextending."

"Fuck… off." I tried to lower the bar, but my arms were shaking so I locked them again.

"Give me the fucking bar, you great redheaded fuckwit."

The battle for possession of the weights didn't last long. Marquis wrenched them from me, then dropped them into the saddle that held the bar when not in use.

My shoulders were on fire. I sat up with a grunt, spun on the bench, and glowered at my best friend. Marquis simply cocked an eyebrow, crossed his arms, and gave me that look of his. It was his highfaluting regal look. He'd perfected it since getting involved with Prince Kaleb.

"What the hell?!" I barked, mad at him for… what exactly? Showing up unbidden, uninvited, and unwanted for starters. "I had everything under control."

"Yep, I could see that. Another ten seconds and you would have been pinned there. Why didn't you call me if you wanted to work out? I'd be happy to spot you."

"I don't need no one hovering over me like a damn nursemaid. I got Phillippe for that."

"Do I look like a motherfucking nanny?" Marquis fired back. I had no interest in bantering with him today. All I wanted was to be left the fuck alone. Why were people so damn set on making me do things the way they wanted?

"What are you even doing here?"

"Your brother called me," he said and handed my crutches to me. I pushed them aside, then lay back down. "No, no way, you're done in here."

"Fuck off. You're not the boss of me." I reached for the bar. He slapped my hands aside. That made me even madder. I reached for the bar again. He took hold of it, pressing down from above as I tried to lift from below. My shoulder complained loudly, the still knitting flesh, muscle, and tendons not at all happy with the leap in dead weight I was asking it to bear.

"Wow, that was a mature comeback. Did you learn that in kindergarten?"

"Let go or I will punch you in the balls," I snarled, putting everything I had into trying to lift the weights. Marquis leaned in more, his biceps flexing, his weight now more than I could move. "Va te faire foutre!"

"Say it in English so I know if I need to whip your freckled ass or not," Marquis barked back.

"Fuck off. Fuck all the fucking way fucking off. Go fuck yourself. And fuck your boyfriend the prince. Go fuck him and his horse. Oh, and fuck the swans too! Fuck everything about you." I punched him in the thigh, hard. I saw him wince, heard his grunt of pain, and the guilt fell down on me like that weight bar was about to. Only the guilt weighed more.

"Ouch, okay, you stand up and we'll take this outside," he parried, lifting his fists, and danced around the bench like a boxer, his feet moving rapidly.

"I can't stand up!" I shouted at the top of my lungs. His fancy footwork slowed, then stopped. "I cannot stand up to punch you in the face. I would like to, though."

"I know."

I sat up and threw my legs to the right. *Leg. Single leg.* He bent down to get my shirt and tossed it into my face before he dropped down on the bench beside me. I didn't wipe my face. Instead, I covered my bare stump from his sight.

"I know you can't stand up right now," he repeated.

"Never. I will never stand up again without help. My pride..."

"Your pride will recover, just like you will." He reached out to grab my knee. My good one, thank God. "You're making this so much harder on yourself than you have to."

I muttered at him in French and then translated. His lips flattened.

"I have never stuck my dick into a mule, just so we're clear," he said before exhaling. "Dunny, man, I know this sucks."

"No, you do not. Sorry, but you saying you know how this feels is bullshit. You can imagine it, but you do not know. No one here knows. You can still play the game you love. You can still walk and dance like Muhammad Ali. You can drive and ski and skate and run. Your boyfriend does not have to look at a scarred, crippled man in his bed. So, no, you know nothing about it!"

He nodded. "Okay, that's fair. I don't know nothing about it. But I *do* know that you're stuck in a dark place and you're scared." I snorted at the comment. Scared. Pfft.

"I'm scared of nothing," I replied, but it sounded weak even to my ears.

"Okay, well then, how about you're worried about an

uncertain future. One that's really different from how you saw your life going. I get that. My dad and uncle battled through the same shit with their medical conditions. Dad was scared shitless when he got his diagnosis. He still is, but he's stopped fighting the doctors and his own damn pride. Now he's accepting help when he needs it. Mostly."

I stared down at my foot. God it was weird not seeing two. I wondered if I would ever adjust.

"I'm not trying to be a jerk, I just am. I get so…" I blew out a mighty breath, "tangled up and so sad for myself. Yes, I know that's selfish, so I get mad at myself for being sad, but then people are all telling me that I'm so lucky. I survived a plane crash. And I should be grateful. Grateful for what? This?" I slapped my stump soundly. "This I am not, nor will I ever be, grateful for."

"I get where you're coming from but, my friend, you are going to hurt yourself more if you don't stop being such a bullhead. The people in your life are trying to help you. Your brother loves you. Your sister-in-law loves you. Your friends love you. Hell, I love you."

"You would not love touching this in bed." I gave the knob where my knee used to be a shake.

"I don't want to touch any part of you. I've seen your ass in the locker room."

That made me snicker a little. "You want my ass. Freckles are hot."

"Sure, if you say so. The point I was making was—"

"I know your point."

"Good. So, the next time you sneak off to work out without a spotter… don't." He knocked his shoulder into mine. "Dumbass. You could have blown out that new shoulder. You like having surgeries?"

"Oui, yes, I love them so much. All the pain and suffering. It makes me hard."

"Figures. You Canadians get stiffies over moose."

"And Americans get boners over eagles."

We sat there side by side for a few minutes, talking about hockey mostly. I'd said all the emotional stuff that I could deal with saying for a while. The door to the gym creaked open, and Cooper stuck his head through the gap. His expression was guarded to say the least. That made me feel shitty too.

"Come in." Marquis got to his feet, then extended a hand to the cute, but wary doctor. "I'm one of Dunny's teammates."

"Ex-teammate. I don't skate anymore," I felt compelled to point out.

"You will someday," Cooper said after giving Marquis a fast, single pump of his hand before turning to me. "If you have a few minutes later, I'd like to talk to you about the fitting processes that we'll be instituting shortly."

"You two go on and talk. I have to get to the barn. Morning skate. You know how coach is about being late." I nodded at Marquis. He clapped my shoulder, said goodbye to Cooper, and told me to call him after the game. Or better yet, come to the game and cheer my team on. That was not happening. It hurt too much, but I lied and said I would think about it. Once he was gone, Cooper stood in front of me, his glasses red framed with black tiger stripes. I'd never seen one person with so many glasses. He must collect them, which is odd, but then again, I collect sports cars, so who was I to say?

"So yeah, about the other day when you were… you know." I waved at the end of my leg, which was now covered with a sweaty T-shirt. "I shouldn't have yelled at you like that."

"No, you shouldn't have, but I understand why you did." He refused to meet my eyes. That made me feel even worse. "I sometimes don't have a good grasp on social cues. Sometimes, I get lost in my world and just do things. Brianna, Uncle Jeremiah, and I had a long talk after the bad incident, and they explained that it's not okay for me to uncover your body parts, look at them, and sketch them when you're not awake to give consent. So, I am sorry for doing that. I won't do it again."

"Thanks. I'm kind of sensitive about people staring at it. I know you're only doing things that are medical. Working out dimensions, measurements, stuff like that to help me get the best fitting prothesis you can make. I shouldn't have been so ugly. I apologize."

"Okay. I accept your apology. So, later today we'd like to get you into the lab with your temporary prosthetic on and see how you do on a treadmill. Nothing too strenuous, just some baseline readings and studying how the fit can be improved over the older one you have. Things of that nature." He did look at me now, waiting for my answer. I bobbed my head. The tension left his jaw. "Good. Maybe after we can swim."

"Okay, yeah, maybe."

He gave me a pen with ladybugs on it. "Why don't ladybugs play hide and seek?"

"I don't know. Why?"

"They always get spotted."

He smiled at me for a fraction of a second. I chuckled. Then, he left without another word. I rolled the pen between my hands for a few minutes, my thoughts wild and windy as the blustery fall day blowing dead leaves down Boston's cobblestone streets.

NINE

Cooper

I LIKED THAT MORAL WAS BACK. HE WAS NOISY AND messy and cursed a lot, but he slotted into my day as if he'd always been there. Dr. Kelly was here as well. The prosthetic expert was now part of my team, but didn't fit in quite as well. She worried a lot and talked a lot. I could see the moments when Moral glazed over while she explained mobility goals in depth. I wanted to tell her to stop talking because even I couldn't concentrate, but I caught Moral's eye, and when he winked, it soothed my frustrated soul. There was something about his eyes—and his face—that made me feel... calm? I couldn't think of the right word, but calm was close enough.

Oh, and horny. That was the other feeling I had, and that was something I tried not to think about too much.

"... walking bars. Okay?"

I tuned back in to silence and realized both Moral and Dr. Kelly were staring at me. Moral looked concerned, Dr. Kelly looked expectant, and I nodded.

"Okay," I agreed because I think that was what they

wanted me to say. Then it was all systems go. The state-of-the-art treadmill was modified with parallel bars, so Moral would have complete support when he attempted to walk with the new prosthetic, and today was day one in a long calendar of things we needed to work on.

"Ready, Moral?" Dr. Kelly asked. Moral nodded and extended his reach to grasp the bars with his strong hands and used that to lever himself to stand from the small bench. Very easily he was upright and gripping the bars. He hadn't put weight on his new prosthetic yet, balancing on his good leg, the foot part of the prosthetic, a small, curved blade, hovering just above the ground. Waiting for a moment, he gingerly connected the blade with the treadmill and slowly eased his body, so it took more weight. I didn't worry that my calculations were wrong—I knew that in theory the tensile strength and curve of the material I'd used was more than strong enough to hold Moral. Only, what if it was too strong, and Moral ended up being unbalanced and unable to use his good leg in the same way? I didn't realize I was holding my breath until I let it out again as Moral was finally steady with his hands on the bars, his good leg strong, and the blade supporting his weight.

"Thoughts?" I asked quickly.

"Are you okay there?" Dr. Kelly spoke at the same time.

Oh yeah, I should ask him first if he's all okay, and then worry about his initial feedback on what he was doing.

"It's all good," Moral murmured and cautiously shifted his weight a little to the right, putting more strain on the blade, before relaxing back. "It's like new skates..." he murmured, and I'm sure that meant something to him because he sent me a smile. "I just need to find my... umm... thing."

"Equilibrium," I offered, and he nodded.

"Okay, can you manage a few steps?"

"Sure," Moral said.

We'd set up the treadmill so it had a setting for Moral to take individual steps, something I'd worked on myself, and something that could probably be rolled out to places dealing with amputees or those paralyzed in accidents. I wanted to see it work completely. I'd need to get the team under Uncle Jeremiah to work on donating units out in the city, and then on to anyone who needed one.

Moral took a step, the bed of the exercise machine moving forward slightly at the shift in his weight—anticipating the step. He stopped after the single action and nodded.

"Okay," he muttered. "That was easy enough." The counter on the screen now showed one, and Dr. Kelly tapped it.

"I want to see fifty there today."

Moral glanced at me, and back to her, and gave a full body sigh. "Only fifty, for fuck's sake, when I used..." He stopped talking and took another step—this time from the blade to his other leg, followed by another to his blade.

The counter showed three and the heart monitor I'd attached to his chest was reading elevated.

"Breathe in and out," Dr. Kelly warned, probably because she'd noticed the elevated reading the same as me. As an athlete in his prime, his resting heart rate was around forty, but his baseline in this test was going to be a lot higher.

"I am fu—breathing," he pointed out and took another two steps.

Five on the reader.

Then he stumbled. It wasn't as if he'd taken another step. It was simply that he'd not landed the blade as accurately as he needed to.

"*T'es donc ben niaiseux!*" he snapped as the muscles in his arms bunched to steady him.

"You're not stupid," I reassured, but he cursed under his breath. "Your center of gravity is different, and you need to be more precise about setting the blade in contact with the ground."

He took another step, and another, and the counter moved from five to nine, then to eleven, thirteen, fifteen, and he stopped. Sweat sheened his skin, and his arms were trembling. I could see that he was allowing his arms to take the strain, and that wasn't going to work for a baseline.

"Stop using your arms to carry your weight. You're messing this up," I instructed as I stared down at the screen.

Silence.

I peered up at Dr. Kelly, who had a face like she'd sucked a lemon, and at Moral, whose eyes were damp with emotion.

Fuck. What had I messed up now? Was I supposed to couch every single thing I said with polite niceties?

"Please?" I added as an afterthought, because please

and thank you went a long way to making people happy. Right?

"I can't do this," Moral muttered, and Dr. Kelly's whole posture slumped.

"Yes, you can," I snapped and moved to stand right in front of him, beyond the screen, and stared right into his tormented eyes. "I want two more steps, and I want you to loosen your arms, shake it off, focus on the blade and on not falling over."

"It's that easy, huh?" Moral observed, and I think he was being sarcastic.

"Yes. If you can do that today, then we can move on to looking at ways to improve what you're doing. If you can't, then we'll have to do the same test tomorrow, and the day after, until I know that you're giving this one-hundred-percent of your focus."

"I am giving this one-hundred-percent," Moral barked, and clearly, sarcasm had moved on to anger.

"Then I want one hundred ten. Loosen your grip on the bars, focus on balance, and give me something to work on."

"I'm not sure this is a good idea," Dr. Kelly intervened, but I pushed ahead.

"Come on, Moral, take the steps."

His eyes narrowed, his jaw tightened, and I thought he might climb off the machine and punch me square on the nose, but instead, he closed his eyes, counting backward from twenty in French, and then he loosened his hold of the bars. Of course, his body weight shifted, and he cursed as he lurched forward, but he caught himself in time, and with his gaze fixed firmly on mine, he inhaled, exhaled, and took a step from good leg to blade, and another from blade and back. This time, his arm muscles weren't bunched up, his knuckles weren't white, and his expression of concentration was intense. He took another two steps, stumbled a little, and then another. I felt weird staring at him, watching him push through all his imagined fears—and all the real fears —and walk on the blade slowly. It was a feeling I'd not felt before, an admiration for what he was achieving, but I wasn't sure that admiration was supposed to make me hard or make me want to climb Moral like a tree.

His lips were parted as he breathed through the steps, his skin damp, the muscles in his legs defined. When I moved out of his sight line to check readings, his ass was just... there. Maybe I was confusing pride in the system I built with pride in how he was doing, or maybe I was just focused all on him. I don't know what it was, but when his steps passed the fifty mark, I let out a whoop at the same time as he stumbled to stop. Having all my readings, I downloaded everything to my tablet, already considering the way that the blade bent to the left by a few millimeters, and the lateral expansion was—

"Earth to Cooper; come in, Cooper."

I blinked back to the here and now. Moral was on the bench, massaging his stump and there was no sign of Dr. Kelly, but the blade was back in its foam container for testing. I had to be clear on what signs of stress there might be and run a full spectral analysis of—

"Earth to Cooper; come in, Cooper."

"Sorry." I yanked myself back to Moral, who looked exhausted. He'd walked on prosthetics before, but this was something entirely new, and it had to have drained his resolve. "Lunch?" I asked because that was next on my list.

"I feel nauseous," Moral admitted after a momentary pause.

"Let's get out of here, up to the roof, and get some air."

He hesitated for a while, and then reached for his crutches. "Sounds like a plan."

We made it to the apartment -- Tony shadowing us -- but we didn't make it to the roof. Instead, as soon as we reached the sofas, Moral slumped into them as if his strings were cut. I could see his stump was reddened, but there was no abrasion, which was a good sign, and clinically, I had all the base data I needed, but he was exhausted.

I fetched him some water, and Tony called down for salads and sandwiches. Moral managed to eat something— at least enough to take some meds—and then he lay back on the sofa. Within a few minutes, his breathing evened out, and he was asleep. I wondered about covering him with a blanket given the apartment was cool and gave into my need to look after him. After I carefully tucked the blanket around him, I watched him sleep for a short time.

"Okay?" Tony asked from my side. I didn't want to be seen staring at Moral because that was just wrong—Tony and Brianna had said that. So I moved away from Moral and sat at the counter.

"I'm all good. Going to check the stats here."

"Okay, I'll be downstairs."

Downstairs in his apartment with his wife and kids, although it was Friday, so I guessed it was a school day.

"Where do your kids go to school?" I called after Tony as he opened the fire stairs with his card.

"Langley Academy. It's a private school, part of the package."

"Oh. Okay. You know, if you wanted to, you could bring them and your wife up here, and we could have a barbecue or something." Like other people did. "The kids would love the pool."

Tony seemed confused, and then nodded.

"Sure thing, boss."

"Not this week though. I haven't thought it through."

"Okay."

"And maybe not next?" I added quickly.

"The one after that, maybe?" He knew me so well.

I contemplated that statement. "That sounds perfect." Two weeks to get myself in the headspace I needed was plenty of time.

He disappeared, and I sat at the counter for so long my ass was numb—and I didn't stare at Moral once.

Well, not for long anyway.

When he stirred a few hours later, I was at his side in an instant.

"Are you okay?"

"Did I fall asleep?" he asked as he glance around. Was he recalling the last time he'd woken up on my sofa and the argument we'd had? I hoped not—I wanted this time to be different.

He closed his eyes again, and after another pause, pushed away the blanket and shuffled to sit upright.

"Can I get you anything?" I asked when he was finally sitting up.

"A drink of water and my bag?"

I fetched both, waiting until he'd swallowed some pills and rested his head on the headrest.

"I need to go back to the apartment," he said. "I should go." He was pressing into the skin above his stump, massaging the area in slow and steady circles. Watching him, mesmerized, I knew I didn't want him to go at all.

Billionaire holds hockey player prisoner.

"You can stay here. Take my spare bed, get some peace and quiet for a while."

"I can't... I have to..." He seemed perplexed, clearly he had a lot of thoughts running through his head, and finally, he nodded. "Okay."

I don't know what it was he'd based his decision on, but I showed him to my room—he didn't need to know that I chose that because it had a better bed—and helped him up. All I could think was that I was thankful I made my bed every morning as part of my routine. Tidy bed, tidy life.

I pulled up the covers and indicated the panel next to the bed. "AC if you need it, lights, drapes, and bottled water in the drawer, which has a small refrigeration unit, so it's cold."

Sitting on the edge of the mattress, I patted his hand, which lay on top of the cover. I could feel the ridge on the hand that was a result of the accident. I traced the scar as gently as I could, and he turned his hand after a while and laced his fingers with mine.

"Thank you for the bed," he mumbled, "and the peace. I'm so fucked right now."

That was my cue to leave, and I untangled my fingers as I stood up.

"Night," I said.

To my absolute horror, some kind of control inside me snapped.

I kissed him goodnight, right on his soft pillowy lips, and stared down at the shock in his expression.

And then, with an embarrassed squeak, I ran.

TEN

Moral

I WAS SHELLSHOCKED.

Mouth open, eyes wide, lips still tingling from that fast, sweet, shy, incredible smooch.

Cooper had kissed me. Right on the lips. While holding my hand.

My brain stuttered and coughed like the first dirt bike I'd ever owned. God above, that old Honda was a total wreck. Rusted, weak in the frame, and with an air filter packed full of dead baby mice. I'd been twelve years old, Phillippe a few years younger, and both of us worked on that rattletrap bike until we had it running and dirt free. Papa had helped, of course, smiling and handing us tools. We'd no sooner got it running, than I had taken my first ride through the woods surrounding our small home. A ride that had cemented my love for the outdoors and for fast things under me, but then my parents had been killed in a car crash. Here one moment and gone the next. Just like that. A snap of the fingers. Two lives snuffed out. Two young boys now orphans.

"I miss you, Papa." I sighed, my fatigue mingling with the shock of being kissed by such a cute and complex man. "And I miss you as well, Mama."

They would have been right next to me, helping me through this, being proud of what I'd achieved today. "Fifty measly fucking steps," I whispered and wondered when exhaustion might turn to pride in what I was achieving. The blade was different, bendier, twisted in odd ways, not solid and unyielding like my first prosthesis, and I hated the feel of it right now. That had to change if I was ever going to be able to skate in circles around a rink.

So tired.

The bedding was thick and soft, the pillow under my head plush. I let my weary head sink into the goose down, inhaling the unique scent of Cooper as sleep overtook me, a tired smile on my lips as I drifted off, thinking of Cooper.

Vallée Rose Tower, the engine has stalled. Repeat, the engine has stalled.

Foxtrot Michael Dundee Paul, can you see the runway yet?

Vallée Rose Tower, non. I cannot see the airfield. The engine has stalled. Repeat, the engine has stalled. I am having a serious situation here.

Foxtrot Michael Dundee Paul, roger that. We have you on radar. What is your airspeed and altitude?

Vallée Rose Tower, my airspeed is one hundred five miles per hour and slowing rapidly. My altitude is three thousand feet and falling quickly.

Foxtrot Michael Dundee Paul, roger that. Pull up on the nose of the plane and bank south-southwest. We will bring you in on the farmland that should be appearing to your left. Do you see the fields yet?

Yes! Yes, Vallée Rose Tower, I do see the fields. The plane is not responsive. Repeat the plane is not responsive. I'm descending at about four hundred feet per minute. Dieu sauve-moi.

Foxtrot Michael Dundee Paul, roger that. Remain calm. Maintain level wings and follow the woodland perimeter. Try to restart the engine. If that does not work, try throttle full forward and mixture idle cut off. Once the engine starts firing, you will have several seconds to add mixture to keep it running. Do you copy, Foxtrot Michael Dundee Paul?

Vallée Rose Tower, negative on the engine restart. Negative on the engine restart. The engine is on fire. Repeat the engine is on fire. I see the fields now. The nose is down but the wings are level. I am going in hard. I am bracing for impact now.

A SCREAM TO WAKE THE DEAD PULLED ME FROM THE hellfire of pain, fear, twisted metal, and the smell of fuel feeding a fire.

Sweat burned my eyes, my heart thundered inside my ribs, and all I could smell was smoke and blood.

A light came on beside me, blinding me, as I rolled from the bed with a thud, my dinner close to reappearing.

"Breathe, breathe, you're safe now."

A shadowy shape knelt down beside me, a cool hand went to my sweaty brow.

I prattled off something in French. A long, muddled string of words that made no sense to my mind. The hand on my brow smoothed back my hair.

Cooper replied to me in that terrible French accent of his. My eyes began to adjust to the light, his face coming into clarity as I lay on my back, blankets tangled around my middle, soaked with perspiration.

"I feel sick," I coughed out. Cooper reached over me and handed me a small trash can. It was empty and smelled of pine. Inside my head, I could see the tips of the pines grabbing at the wheels of the plane as I hurtled toward a field of cornstalks. Pine trees snapping and breaking, boughs catching fire, the smell of pine wood and crisp electrical bits entering my nose. I emptied my stomach into the trash can, heaving until nothing remained. Cooper sat beside me, hair a knotted mess, purple framed glasses sitting on his tiny nose at an angle, his feet bare, his pajama bottoms pushed up to his knobby knees. "Sorry, sorry, so sorry. That is weak of me."

"Don't be absurd. Being sick isn't a weakness. Can you sit up?" He grabbed my biceps.

"*Let go!* I can do it alone!" I barked in English, hauling myself up and shoving the blankets down to cover my bared stump. He sat back on his heels, looking wounded. "I am sorry. Please. Forgive my rudeness. You were only trying to help."

"I'm sorry for acting as if you were helpless. You could probably bench press this bed with one hand and me with the other."

I rested my back against the bed as I pulled in long, deep gulps of air. "The bed, probably; you, yes, for sure."

He pushed the dirty trash can away and sat beside me, easing his thin legs under the covers, his chilly toes brushing over the skin of my thigh, then tickling the side of my stump as he settled in beside me.

"Do the dreams come often?" he asked after a moment or two passed. I nodded, and he reached over me to pull open a drawer on his bedstand. He pulled a notebook covered with ladybugs out from the drawer. "I shall jot that down." Removing a sleek red pen from the coils, he began to scribble madly, his tongue between his teeth, sleep-knotted hair tumbling into his eyes. "Are they the same dreams?"

"Mostly, yes. About the crash. My counselor says it is a form of PTSD. He says it is common after such an ordeal, depression too, but usually, over time, survivors begin to feel a great sense of self-esteem as they battle through the psychological and physical aftereffects of the trauma. I'm having my doubts."

"Well," he glanced up from his notes, "it *has* only been a few months. I'm relatively sure that given time to heal mentally and physically, you'll experience growth. I read about a study of airplane crash survivors that stated they scored better on several standardized tests dealing with emotional distress than those who fly but have never been involved in a crash. Perhaps with time, you'll find yourself growing in terms of deeper inner strength; a deeper, stronger sense of spirituality; and deepening personal relationships."

"Hmm, a new appreciation of life, eh?"

"Yes, exactly." He went back to his notes, mumbling to himself. My arms and legs were still rubbery, but my racing pulse had quieted.

"You kissed me," I tossed out. His head whipped up and those magnificent chocolate eyes of his flared. He peeked to the side. "I'm not complaining. I liked it. It gave me a nice few hours' sleep. I think I was smiling when I drifted off."

His cheeks grew red. "I don't usually do that. Kiss men. Even broad-shouldered, red-haired men. I do like gingers though. And freckles. And strong guys who like to cuddle."

"I would like to do that very much." His eyes met mine, his pen paused over the page now filled with his thoughts and observations. "Cuddle. When I have the bad dreams at home, I cuddle with Penelope."

"Is that your girlfriend?" He stared at me, worry knitting his brow.

"It is my dog. She is a basset hound. So sweet. I miss her badly."

"Oh. A dog. Umm. Dogs are nice. She'll help you recover." He said it so primly as if his mind had already willed it into being, and so, it would be done. And probably it would be. People seemed to jump and ask "How high?" for Cooper. "Will she bite?"

"A biting basset. Hmm. I've never heard of one. She is super sweet. You will love her to bits and pieces."

"Good. Then we'll get her here as soon as we can. I've never had a dog before. I think it will be good for you." He smiled at me, cheeks round as apples, hair still a wild mess. "Then you can cuddle with her at night."

"But what about tonight?"

His smile faded, replaced with a rush of pink to his cheeks that spread to the tip of his nose. God, he was cute. So small and unpretentious.

"We could cuddle. If you want," he whispered.

"Yes, please, I think I'd like that." I reached for him, sliding my hands under his arms, lifting him and his notebook. He made a squeaky mouse sound right before I placed him on my lap. Without prompting, he burrowed into my chest, his notebook open, his head resting on my shoulder. The scarred one. His cheek was right on the raised hard incision mark, and he never flinched at all. I pressed a kiss to his hair, snuggling him tightly to my chest, inhaling his warm, sleepy cinnamon smell.

We sat there on the floor, talking, cuddling, and drawing ladybugs among his notes for two hours. My ass was numb, but my heart was full. And the dream had faded away into that far-off place where all bad dreams ended up.

———

A WEEK LATER, I HAD MY OWN FLOOR IN THE CAHTECH building.

One whole floor. For me, Phillipe, Yuka, her twin brother Piita Kalluk -- who was one heck of a hockey player in his own right and played for the Manitoba Junior Hockey Association, and was being scouted big time by several teams, including the Rebels -- and of course my sweet Penelope. That, on any given day, would be enough people and pets for the massive living space we now had.

But today, for some reason, my brother thought it would do me good to have a "few" friends over for dinner. Few meaning ten or so Rebels. They weren't playing today, and so Phillippe had told them all to come and bring a dish to pass. Yuka made sure to have plenty of good food on hand when they arrived. Which turned out to be good, as the guys ended up bringing football food aka wings, pizza, and beer.

"You should eat the chicken breasts that I made," Yuka scolded with humor as I chomped on another slice of everything pizza.

"I'll eat that tomorrow. I promise," I replied, giving her my most pitiful look. "I've been eating healthy all week. Between you and Dr. Kelly comparing nutrition notes, and Cooper shoving celery sticks at me every time he sees me, I'm tired of being good. Just this one day, I promise."

She gave me that maternal eye. She was a lovely woman with long, black hair and a broad nose, smart as a whip, and tough as nails. Her brother, Piita, was just as pretty. Phillippe and Yuka had met three years ago when my doofus brother tried to jump his bike off the roof of my cabin into the small pond beside my home. He'd broken his arm, and she had been the ER nurse on duty. Charming as we Dunkirks are, he soon won her heart and married her last summer up in Rankin Inlet, Nunavut, where she and her family are from.

"I'll be keeping a watch on your weight," she chided, then patted Penelope's head while the dog lounged on my lap. Having her here had done wonders for my mood. And it made me get up when I didn't want to and walk her. Dogs are gifts from God. "You know that the PT for your new prosthetic will be as hard, if not harder, than training camp."

"Oh shit, Dunny, I thought you'd be sitting around with your foot up," Marquis said, flopping down on my left, with a slippery chicken wing and a small helping of tossed salad—Yuka insisted—on his plate.

"Ha. Funny. Foot." I sighed and rolled my eyes.

"I heard you and the recluse are cracking jokes day and night." He placed his plate on the coffee table, shook open a paper napkin, and laid it just so on his lap to protect his shiny plum trousers. Even at a low-key dinner, the man was fashionable.

"Yeah, we do. He's not afraid to say the wrong thing." I rubbed a hand over Penelope's head. She sighed in her sleep, drool leaking out of her jowls, soaking the leg of my fleece workout pants.

"Hey, I was looking for the guest of honor," Xander said, pecking Yuka on the cheek before sitting down on my other side to fuss over my dog. "And here she is. Hello, Penelope. Who's a good girl? Who's the prettiest girl ever? *You are!* Yes, you are."

Penny loved the attention. Her tail thumped as her brown eyes opened just a little.

I chuckled at Xander. When Phillippe had first announced his grand idea of this dinner, I'd balked. The guys hadn't seen me for a few months. When they'd last talked to me, it was while I was in hospital, because I sure as shit didn't talk to them after the game where I'd been in the owner's box. I'd been pretty much out of it in the hospital, awash in bitter depression and pain, hopped up on pain meds… I'd been a mess.

Now it was late October, and I was less of a mess. Externally.

Internally?

That was a work in progress. I'd become super introverted during my recovery time. Preferring to spend my time with my brother, his wife and her brother, and my dog. Other people stared. They offered pity and remorse. Or, like so many did, they would shy away from the cripple with the scars. So, I shut down and hid, and still was, if I was being honest. I'd ruffled up like a wet hen at my brother when he'd told me we were having company. I was happy to be here with just Dr. Kelly and Cooper. And Penelope, of course. Funny how Cooper had just been accepted by my heart. He never winced or gasped or pulled away from my scars or stump.

Yesterday, I had allowed him to touch it so he could get measurements for the prosthetic. Only him. No one from his team. Just him. He smiled and talked about silly things like space jokes—he'd run out of one-legged ones it seemed—or how beneficial ladybugs were, or how he'd been arguing with Neil deGrasse Tyson about which planet in our solar system was the prettiest. He'd been gentle with my limb as he worked, his mouth running all the while he measured this way and that. His fingers were soft, his touch firm, not shy or tentative.

"… about him coming. He's rooming with Austin and Robbie until the rental the team lined up is ready."

I snapped out of the memory of Cooper's hand on my bare thigh. Marquis was nibbling at his wing, while Xander stared at me in expectation of a reply.

"Sorry. I drifted. Long day in the pool, then with the

physical therapist." I rubbed my face, my fingers finding thick red stubble. I'd not shaved for a few days. Ever since Cooper had offhandedly mentioned that he would like to someday kiss a man with a beard to see if it tickled. Give me a week or two, and I'd have enough whiskers to show him how ticklish it could be. We kissed a lot. Never anything too wild, but yeah, his lips were soft as pillows and usually tasted of something sweet he'd just—

"… think they'd bring him."

I blinked back at the man talking to me. "Sorry, did it again."

"It's cool. You're working hard." Xander patted my shoulder softly, as if he were scared to give it a good knock like he would've before. I sighed internally. "I was talking about Lomac being here. I know that must sting."

Oh. Right. Logan Mackie. Standing over there by my sliding glass door, drinking my beer, eating my food, joking with my friends, and playing my position. Also, why did he have to be so damn good-looking? Could he not have a few scars? He was a hockey player, for fuck's sake.

"Nah, it's fine. I'm good with it. Not like I'll ever be back in a Rebels jersey. All part of the business, yeah? Good on him. Happy for him. Yep. Good on him." I watched both men glance at each other, then smile in unison at me. "I mean, yeah, of course, it's not easy, but I'm fine. Good. Happy. Feeling great!"

"Good, good, glad you're dealing with everything so well," Marquis said before wiping his saucy fingers on a wet wipe. "Phillippe said you were having some trouble before, with depression, but I told the team that Dunny wouldn't be down for long. You're a force, my friend."

"Yeah, a force for sure. You'll be running circles around us before you know it!" Xander tossed out.

"Totally. Yeah. Circles." I grinned at them, my fingers moving steadily over Penelope's long back. I never once stopped petting her the entire time they were there. It was only after the team had left and I was in my bed ready for sleep, my family retired to their rooms—sans Piita, who had gone out with Austin, Robbie, and Logan for some young guy fun on the town—that I could release the rictus smile that I'd held all night long.

I lay in bed with Penelope at my side, her floppy ears spread over my hand, and stared at the ceiling. Above me were Tony and his family. The building was incredibly well built, and no noise ever seeped down from the children. Above that would be Cooper's private quarters. I wondered what he was doing, if he was working on my prosthetic, or if he was asleep. No sooner had I thought of him, a text came in from a few floors above. I smiled an honest smile when I read what he had sent.

WHERE WOULD AN ASTRONAUT PARK HIS SPACESHIP? A parking meteor. ~C

SEVERAL LAUGHING EMOJIS FOLLOWED. I HIT HIM BACK while snorting madly. Man, I was a sucker for silly jokes and nerdy men.

. . .

Funny stuff, Doc! Thanks for the laugh. Wish you would have been here tonight. ~M

Too many people for me. I'm happier away from dinner parties. ~C

You could have told them good jokes. They meant well. I'm sad now. Seeing them all. Knowing I'm not one of them anymore. This sucks. SIGH. Sorry. Don't mind me. ~M

Don't be sorry. Being sad over things lost is normal. You want me to come down? I have Mallow bars. Don't tell Brianna. ~C

Yeah, a Mallow bar sounds good. I'll meet you at the front door. Mind the watch dog. She slobbers her hello. ~M

I remember. See you in five. ~C

"We have company coming. Be good, and don't slobber on his toes. He didn't like that last time," I reminded my dog as I threw off the covers and picked up my crutches.

Cooper was at the door when I got there, a box of Mallow bars in one hand, an old DVD of *The Goonies* in the other. Penelope wagged and snuffled and drooled.

"Perfect," I said, brushing his lips with mine. He sighed, leaning in and going up to his toes for another peck. The man *really* enjoyed kissing.

"What? The treats or the movie?" he asked in a whisper.

"Everything. All of it. You."

ELEVEN

Cooper

"I THINK I SHOULD GO ON A DATE."

Brianna stopped stirring the gravy and stared up at me with her mouth open.

"I'm sorry?"

"A date. With a man. Or a woman. Although, I think I prefer men. Not that I have a lot to go on, what with the fact that I've only ever cuddled one person. Moral. And I loved it, but is that because I've never done that with anyone else? I mean, I need to go out, date, cuddle some more, have… y'know…"

"Y'know?"

Was it just me or did Brianna sound really confused? She wasn't even watching the gravy. She'd always told me she never took her eyes off it, which made it the best gravy ever. I mean, it was really good gravy, and I was hungry, so maybe now wasn't a good time for this chat, but this was my fixed Sunday with her, Uncle Jeremiah, and Brianna's family, and I wanted to chat informally, outside the office. I couldn't believe only four weeks had passed since the last Sunday dinner, but everything had changed so much. Moral Dunkirk made me want things I'd never considered, like companionship, trust, friendship, kissing, sex… lots of kissing and sex, maybe.

Brianna was just staring at me, and I swear there was a burning smell, and maybe I wasn't making any sense—wouldn't be the first time.

"S.E.X.," I added for clarity. She continued to stare at me until she obviously caught the burning scent and took the pan off the stove with a soft curse. "Sorry."

"It's okay," she grumbled. "I have store bought that I can use instead, if I have to—start again."

"Well, a date might lead to sex, and then, I won't be so…" Ridiculously pathetic that I'd made it to twenty-seven and was still a virgin. I mean, who did that?

"I think you need to sit down," she finally offered and waved at the stool. She poked her head outside the kitchen door, called for Uncle Jeremiah, and explained dinner would be late. "Start from the beginning."

The beginning? I could do that, and I cracked my neck and recalled everything. "Well, my first memory was from when I was three. I mean, experts say on average that kids have first memories at four, but—"

"Not *that* kind of beginning, Cooper. I mean, tell me why you want to date."

"Oh, okay. Well, most people want to date, right? Like, I mean, get a boyfriend or a girlfriend or more than one, sometimes more than one at the same time. I missed out on most of the normal stuff, and I know for a fact that some people don't want relationships, but statistically—and I have numbers to back this up—most people feel the urge to connect with someone else, right?"

"And that is what you want to do?"

"Yes, that's what I'm saying. I have this urge."

Jeremiah sauntered into the kitchen as confused as Brianna, although his confusion was more likely to be around the burnt gravy.

"What's going on?" he asked, taking the stool next to me.

"Urge?" Brianna ignored Uncle Jeremiah and forged ahead. "You make it sound like a disease."

I sighed dramatically. "It feels like a disease right now because it's confusing and messy, and..." I fussed with the strap of my watch, with a million conflicting synapses firing in my thoughts. Dating through school and college was impossible and improbable. I was either wildly younger than my cohorts as I was pushed through education, or I had my head buried so deep in books that I likely missed every chance a connection could have presented itself. "Socially awkward" was the tag I earned at school as I flew through the years. Autism was the label I wore at the doctor's office. Orphan was the mark on the legal files attached to my estate. "Most likely to save the world" was the title my peers in college gave me. I was Rain Man, I was Einstein, and all of it rolled off me like water off a duck's back because none of it mattered as long as I could do my experiments and discover things that were new to the world. Somewhere in all those labels, I never collected the one that was *boyfriend*.

"What's messy, sweetheart?"

Emotion caught in my throat as all those thoughts, plus Brianna's quiet compassion, made my chest tight.

"I function socially," I said with careful precision. No one could say I was perfect in every social situation, but Brianna was there to help, and Uncle Jeremiah was just as much a barrier to the real world, and then there was Tony —the one with the family I'd never even met. Meeting Moral, though, meant I had situations that didn't involve anyone else, but me and him, and I was at a loss to know what was best to do.

I told jokes, and he smiled. We cuddled and kissed, but did that make us something more than just friends?

"Did you hear the joke about the fourteen-year-old spectrum kid and the jock?" I deadpanned, even though the words were fraught with emotion. "Turns out the joke was on me when he told me that kissing me was just a stupid bet."

"You never told me that." Uncle Jeremiah seemed shocked. There was a lot I didn't tell him, from the crying to the bullying, right up to the fact that my revenge on the jock had left him with no body hair after I switched his shampoo -- and a permanent prom record of said lack of hair. No one knew it was me—or at least, I didn't get anyone asking me what I'd done. But that's science for you. No one expects the weird kid to have the skills to get quiet revenge on the wannabe prom king.

Brianna closed her eyes and, then, came around the counter to hug me. "Sweetheart," she whispered, and her hug was my undoing because a huge rush of emotion overwhelmed me and tears slipped out of my eyes, dampening her sweater. I don't know how long I stood there, all hugged up by the woman I thought of as Mom now, with Uncle Jeremiah hugging me from the other side.

Slowly, my need for space reasserted itself and the hugging became too much, so I slipped away from them. They didn't stop me. I made it all the way around the counter and leaned there with the barrier between us.

"So, I've been kissing Moral, which is highly unethical because the results of the experiment are no longer valid."

"Moral isn't a science project," Brianna said with a soft smile.

"How can I get perspective on this when I'm hugging him and kissing him and wanting all kinds of other stuff with him? It doesn't make sense. I mean, I have the science side, wanting to create a new product that will help people—but all I want to do is to create it for him just to make him smile because sometimes he's so sad. Then I think, what if I'm doing this wrong? So, the me side, the one in here…" I pressed a hand to my temple and then to my chest, "is all upside down."

"So you want to date someone else to experience it?" Brianna summarized.

"He does?" Now it was Uncle Jeremiah's turn to be shocked. "You do?"

"I think if I had a benchmark to qualify all these…" I patted my belly this time, which is where permanent butterflies live, "feelings in here, then maybe I could do better with Moral? Maybe get perspective, maybe get back on track."

"No," Brianna said with that tone she used when I was planning on doing something crazy. Like the time I wanted to test the bat wings I'd created off the penthouse floor. I was convinced that with only a two percent margin of error that I would land in Boston Common. She was one-hundred-percent convinced that I'd end up killing myself.

"No, I shouldn't date?"

"Yes," Uncle Jeremiah agreed, which confused me.

"Yes, I shouldn't date because you agree with my comment to Brianna, or yes, I should?"

"You should have a date with Moral and see how you get along." Brianna picked up another saucepan and waggled it at me—not as a threat, at least I don't think so. "Random dates won't show you anything unless you have a connection, even one as messy as the one you have with Mr. Dunkirk."

"So, I need to have a date with Moral, not random other people to practice."

"Yep," Uncle Jeremiah added.

"Okay then."

Which is how I found myself, three weeks later, standing outside Moral's door with flowers and a box of chocolates. We were going on a date, and I was picking him up from his apartment and taking him to the best place I knew—my apartment, where I'd hired in this awesome chef and staff, who'd made the patio into a wonderland of twinkling lights.

I heard some shouting behind the door. The small family that Moral had living with him, Phillippe, his wife Yuka, and Piita, were loud and funny -- and not one of them told me my jokes were stupid -- but they spent a lot of time being rude to each other. Penelope was woofing softly, and there appeared to be chaos behind the door.

Dunny! You smell pretty!

Dunny! Condoms!

Asshole!

Heat flushed my entire body, and I squirmed. Condoms were in my bathroom drawer, along with the top ten varieties of lube, as suggested by an Advocate article entitled "30 Liquid Assets Every Gay Man Should Know." It basically said that gay sex was a wonderland of fluids, liquids, lotions, and lubes and that a smart bottom was basically a chemist. I wasn't sure if I was a bottom, or a top, or whatever, still I had everything they listed, plus wipes and towels, ready for date five or whenever sex might happen, if we even get to date five. I'd ticked off everything, just in case, but tonight was about a date, and not all dates ended in sex.

Well, that was according to Brianna, who was openly concerned as the days went by, that I wasn't in full control of my libido.

She was probably right. Having a technical brain like mine and craving isolation didn't mean that I didn't want messy, wonderful, slick, squirmy brain-melting orgasms— hell, I'd managed quite an impressive record of them all on my own—but to have that with another person just scared the ever-loving shit out of me.

I just wanted to be with Moral. Alone. With some more kissing and cuddles, and to have it be officially my first date.

The door finally opened after some more shouting, and there he was, all dressed up in a pale blue shirt and dark tie, with black pants and the right pant leg pinned up. He'd tidied his beard, brushed and styled his hair, and he was red in the face.

"My family are all assholes," he complained as he crutched out of the door, shushing Penelope back from it, and awkwardly pulled it shut behind him. "Condoms," he added under his breath.

"It's okay, I have them," I explained because, clearly, it was an issue. "Do you want to tell them?"

"God. No." He was all wide-eyed and bear-like, and I just wanted to kiss him. So I did. Briefly. With the flowers and chocolates squashed between us until I stood back and thrust them at him.

"For you," I explained, and for a moment, we stared at each other, then at the flowers, the box, and then at his knee and his crutches, and finally our gazes met at the top. "Oops." I really hadn't thought this through. He still needed both hands on his crutches, so I knocked on the door of his apartment and Phillippe answered immediately, which led me to believe he'd been right behind it waiting. "Can you take these?" I asked, and he took the flowers and chocolates and smiled at me. "Also, I have condoms, so you don't need to worry."

Phillippe made a face like he was sucking lemons, or trying not to laugh, and then he nodded in all seriousness.

"Don't eat my chocolates!" Moral snapped as the door closed and he turned to me. "They'll eat all my chocolates," he mourned.

I patted his muscled arm. "I'll get you some more. Ready?"

We headed for the elevator, and I keyed in the code to get to my floor. We rode in silence upward, but I didn't think it was a weird silence. I bet Moral was just relieved that I had the condoms so his family wouldn't worry, but when the doors opened into my lobby and we moved out, he caught me with a cautious touch to my elbow, balanced precariously on his crutches.

"I don't want you to think that all I want is that."

"That what?" I blinked at him, and then it hit me. S.E.X. "Oh no, it's all good, statistically sex comes after date five. I researched it."

He nodded. "Well, okay then."

We made our way through the apartment and to the few stairs that took us to the roof.

"Maybe I should have set this up down here? It's not fair that you have to get up the stairs on a date, I should—"

"It's all good." He maneuvered up the twelve steps with careful precision, seeming stronger than the first day I met him. Soon he'd have his first experimental prothesis, but I made a mental note that I needed to work in the dynamics of climbing stairs, as much as I did on the subtleties of creating something that meant Moral could maybe skate a little.

He stopped when we reached the patio, taking in the waiter who stood by the table, the lights that reflected on the cutlery, and the candles in the middle of the table.

"Wow!" he exclaimed.

"I know you like barbecue, so I got Chef Lombardi from The Grill to create us something. I'm sorry I can't take you *out* out, but I get too much attention, and I wanted it to be just us and—"

He kissed me to stop me talking, which was fine by me, only we needed to sit and eat, so I eased away, and waved for him to choose a seat.

"So, tell me about your family." I selected from my list

of questions that I'd researched as ice breakers on dates. It was enough for Moral to entertain me with stories of his childhood with Phillippe, how the hockey team were like his family, how much he missed them, and his worries that he was pushing them away. By the time we'd eaten the very best steak I'd ever tasted, with all the side dishes I could imagine, he'd run out of things to say and turned the question back on me.

"So, tell me about yours," he asked and sipped on a bright green key lime mocktail expectantly.

"It's on Wikipedia, and there's a documentary, you know," I gave my standard reply.

"I've never looked you up on Wiki or seen a documentary on you," he said and picked out a wedge of fruit to suck.

When did someone sucking on fruit make me so hard?

"Oh, okay, well, Mom and Dad, my biological parents," I qualified that if I ever had to explain, "were volcanologists, renowned experts in their field. I was eight when they died in an eruption... it was quick. I was on a far ridge with Uncle Jeremiah, part of the support team, I guess. Taking measurements, that kind of thing. I talked to Mom, and she was excited. She was the geochemist part of the team and there were indications in melt inclusion data to suggest... you don't need to know that. Anyway, the volcano took them, and Uncle Jeremiah took me, and we were lucky to get away. Discovery did a documentary on my parents and the volcano, last pictures of them moments before disaster and all that, but I've never watched it. Ironically, the Coopersil fabric I created might have saved them if they'd managed to climb high enough, but they were too low down and would've never made it out. It was quick, and that's good."

I couldn't get a read on Moral's expression, but I didn't think there was pity there, maybe compassion, understanding, but whatever it was, he didn't ask me more questions.

He simply held my hand under the twinkling lights, and we ate a decadent chocolate dessert that melted under the hot sauce.

And it was perfect.

TWELVE

Moral
——————

I'D BEEN AROUND THE BLOCK A TIME OR TWO.

Heck, maybe I'd circled that block three times.

In all that time, and with all those lovers, I'd never felt a connection as I did with Cooper. It went far beyond getting my rocks off. Hell, it had been so long since I'd had sex, I wasn't sure I remembered how. And if I could dredge up the basics, who would want to lie with a man who looked like me?

Cooper. Cooper would. Cooper *did*. He was sending out strong signals that I wasn't sure he realized he was emitting. We'd kissed, sure, and touched, always above the waist. He knew my chest well and had a fascination with my abs, as well as the red curls covering my chest and belly. He also liked to kiss and cuddle. All things that I was totally on board with. Holding him tight was everything to me. His slight weight on my lap, the touch of his lips to mine, the gentle caress of his slim hands over my arms and back were tethers. His attraction and affection kept me going when I wanted to give up. He was a slight man, but he gave no quarter.

He didn't baby me or let me slide as my brother was prone to do. He simply told me in kind, but firm, tones that if I didn't get my ass into PT, I'd never get back to being the Moral I used to be. Blunt, yet compassionate. It worked for me. *He* worked for me. I wanted more time with him. More sharing, more laughter, more touches, more whispered secrets. I was falling in love with him.

"… orbiting bodies comets follow Kepler's Law, the closer they are to the sun the faster they move."

I drifted back from the foggy land of realization to drop smack dab into a running dissertation from the man that I was crazy about. Shit. What was he talking about? Comets. Stars. Space. Cool. Yeah, the final frontier. I glanced from him to the night sky.

"There are too many lights in Boston to see the stars very well. I should take you home. I sometimes lie on the dock at my lake house and watch the night sky. So many falling stars! And now is the best time to see the Northern Lights. We should go now."

He leaned up, his pink framed glasses—I had come to learn he had several dozen pairs that he left lying all over everywhere—resting on his cute little button nose, his dark eyes wide with wonder.

"To Canada?"

I nodded, picking at the remains of a baked potato on my plate. "Yes, to Quebec, to Vallée Rose. Fall is past now, sadly, but perhaps there will be snow falling. In November, it snows usually. The lake will be cold, but not frozen yet, and the night skies clear. We could ride a snowmobile into the woods to the highest peak of the mountain range that cradles Vallée Rose and set up a telescope. You could watch the heavens, and I could cook us some stew on a fire. Then, we could go to our tent and snuggle up in a sleeping bag as the Northern Lights turn the night sky shades of greenish-yellow, red, and blue."

I pulled my sight from the city skyline.

He smiled softly, his gaze wondrous. "I would love that."

"But?" I shoved my plate aside. One of the chef's assistants cleared it away and quickly replaced it with a dish holding a hearty slab of cheesecake with raspberry topping.

"But I'm not a fan of traveling." He winced a bit at his confession. "And you're not able to ride a snowmobile yet. You need to devote more time to PT, and you've been slacking."

"Oui, I have," I admitted, poking at the crust of my dessert. "I am afraid of moving so fast in my recovery that when I get my new bionic leg, you'll be done with me." I glanced up to find him staring at me as if I were speaking some long dead language. Latin or something. Well, he probably knew Latin. His accent would be atrocious, but he could probably speak it.

"Why would I be done with you?" He seemed genuinely confused.

"Because when I am well, your scientific interest in me will end. I'll go my way and you will go yours," I put my fork down, "I do not wish to have that happen because I want to be around you more—when I'm healthy and whole again."

"You're whole now, Moral." I scoffed. He reached over the table to still my hand as I cut into my cheesecake. I looked up, and his gaze captured mine. "You are the most masculine man I have ever known. Strong and funny and furry. You're perfect as you are. A prosthetic won't make you more of a man because you're already as manly as a man can be."

"You are lovely to say that." I thought to mention that his adoration of my manliness might be skewed, as he'd never really been with another man. Or woman, if I was reading him right, and I was rather sure that I was. "So you want to date me after you're done with my leg?"

"Of course. There will be years of follow-up research to be done."

"Oh."

He gave my hand a squeeze. "That wasn't kind. It's not what I meant. I mean, it was what I meant, but I should have prefaced it by saying that I find myself feeling..." he blew out a breath that puffed his cheeks, "I'm feeling... you make me feel... I want to date you. Hard."

That made me chuckle. "Ah, well, hard dating. I like the sound of that."

"Yes, as do I! Hard dating. Can we have sex now?" I choked on a mouthful of cheesecake. "Sorry. Was that too direct? I have lube and condoms."

"Yes, we covered that earlier. I just wasn't sure if you were really into wanting to do things like that. You seem so happy to cuddle. And if that is all that you would ever want, then I would be happy with that too. What I feel for you..." I scrabbled for the right word in English. "It is overwhelming in its vastness."

"That was eloquent." He left his seat and plopped his backside onto my lap. With a soft purr of contentment, he snuggled in tight, his tiny ass on my thighs, his hip tilted and rested against what was rapidly becoming a rousing erection. "I like the way you smell and feel, and that your penis is hard already. That's a good sign."

"A good sign?" I slid my arms around him, trying to lift him off my dick, but he was having none of that.

"Yes, that we're sexually compatible." He kissed me softly, his tongue darting out to touch mine in a way that sent jolts of want coursing through me. The softness of his lips and the sweet taste of raspberry topping—which he ate, but left the cheesecake, but no worries I would eat it as soon as I got done with mine—pulled a soft rumble of desire out of me.

"I'd say we are compatible," I panted several minutes later, my cock throbbing, his lips puffy and slick. The server had disappeared, thank God, but had left the cheesecake. Cooper shivered. "We need to go inside. It is too cold out here for you. You're not a stout Québécois like me."

"Let's go to bed. I want to fool around."

He stood and offered me his hand. I was smiling at the old-fashioned term. It fit the man, though. "Grab the desserts. I will want some after we fool around."

"Okay." He scooped up both dishes and waited for me to get up, balanced, and get my crutches under my arms. We stepped inside, glad for the warmth it brought to his cheeks, and he pushed the door shut behind me with his foot. "Go to my room. I want to dismiss the chef and his helper. Then we can have sex time, followed by dessert."

"I would say that feasting on your slim body would be the sweetest treat ever."

His cheeks flamed, but his eyes -- oh those dark eyes -- lit up. I hurried as fast as a man on crutches can hurry, finding his massive bedroom dimly lit. He seemed to like nightlights on in his rooms after dark. I had just lowered myself to the bed and placed my crutches against the copper headboard when he arrived, his hands carrying two plates of dessert, his lower lip caught between his teeth.

"If you're having second thoughts, we do not have to do anything other than kiss and cuddle. I meant it when I said that would make me happy. It is you who I adore."

"No, no, I want to do sexy things with you. I just... well." He padded over, placed the platters of dessert on the nightstand, and stood in front of me, placing his hands on my face and lifting my sight from the noticeable bulge in his trousers upward. I could see the passion banked in his brown eyes. "I think I just realized how big you are. You take up so much of my bed. Heck, you fill the room! And I love that, but then my mind went to the size of your penis, which in proportion would be rather large as well as you're large. And then I began worrying if my body could accommodate such a monumental appendage. Of course, the human body *does* have remarkable elasticity. Just look at how a woman's—"

"Cooper, take a breath." He drew in a long gulp of air. "Now let it out through your nose." He did as I instructed, his shoulders dropping some as he exhaled. "Good. Okay, so while I am deeply pleased that you think my prick is so enormous—"

"It's girthy. I've been sitting on it or wiggling against it for several weeks now."

"Yes, I'm aware." If he only knew how many times I had jerked off after our kiss and cuddle sessions, he'd be stunned. "But it's not *that* big. Normal for a man my size. But we're not going to rush into anything. So please, do not worry. Now kiss me."

His lips curled at the edges, and he placed his mouth on mine. I licked in deep, gathered him close, and rolled us over to our sides in one fast motion. He snorted in amusement, the rush of air leaving him and bursting into my mouth. I inhaled it, stroked his tongue with mine, and then set about slowly removing his shirt.

He squirmed about like a worm, his hands roaming over my head and shoulders, his legs scissoring as our kisses grew hotter and wetter.

"Oh gosh, I like this a lot," he gasped when I had his chest bared and was flicking his tight little nipples with my thumbs. "Oh! That's amazing. Can we touch dicks? I saw a movie where they did that."

I drew back just a bit, amused at the notion that my sweet little Cooper had watched gay porn. Also, the thought of his cock pressed to mine had me on the edge instantly.

"Have you been watching porn?" I asked, letting my hand trail down his belly. The muscles twitched. His chest was sparsely dotted with dark hairs, the path to his groin coming in a little thicker the lower I went. "It's okay if you have. Everyone does."

"I peeked a little. Just for research purposes of course." He went to his back, offering himself up to me with complete trust. I took a tiny nipple in my mouth, sucked on it until he was coated with a fine sheen of sweat, and then went to work on his fly. The slick head of his dick emerged from his briefs. My mouth watered, but I went slow, easing him up and out of his pants. His eagerness to divest himself of his slacks made things go a bit more slowly. I kissed his belly, way low, just under his navel.

"Relax, breathe, we've got all night," I whispered across his skin. He giggled and gasped, his hands falling to his sides. Then he was nude, his cock standing at attention, dark brown curls at the base of a sleek, perfect dick. I stroked his thighs, his knees, and his hipbones, skipping his leaking dick entirely. His ragged huffs set my skin on fire.

"Roll to me," I urged, wiggling up on the bed a bit as I tugged on my zipper. He was all over that, moving to face me, then unzipped my fly with haste and helped me free myself of my clothes right down to ridding me of my sock. He wet his lips as he studied my cock.

"You're uncut," he softly said, as if in awe of an uncircumcised prick.

"And you are cut," I answered, slipping a hand between us to cradle his dick and mine. He gasped and purred, his eyes fluttering closed behind his glasses. I held us like that, letting him adjust to a strange hand—and dick —resting by and encircling his cock. "You are so pretty. Delightful. Just as I imagined."

"You are too. Oh you too!" He was so expressive and honest. I loved that about him. "Can we do this?" He placed his hand over mine and began stroking and squeezing our cocks. A shudder ran through me. So much pleasure. He rubbed his thumb over the head of my cock, peeling back the foreskin with a whimpering little sound that went right to my balls. "I like your cock. I like foreskin."

"Yay for… foreskin," I panted, unable to slow the orgasm that was slowly building. I stole a few more kisses, my body on the precipice, but tumbled over the side just as Cooper exploded all over our joined hands. He came with a small groan of pleasure that I would carry with me forever. It was the most glorious sound I'd ever heard. Bodies trembling, hearts thundering, cocks surging, we found completion together.

"I loved that." He sighed as the tremors slowed. He moved over me, pressing my shoulder to the bed, his lips moving over mine. I cupped his tight ass with my sticky hand, smearing our spend over his buttock as his tongue swirled around mine. "Can we do more? I have all those condoms and lubrication. We should do more, I think."

I couldn't help but chuckle. He looked at me through terribly smudged glasses, his cheeks rosy from sex and my whiskers.

"I think we should too, but maybe *after* some cheesecake?"

He blushed even redder, then kissed me for all he was worth. Which was a lot. We rolled around the bed, making out, touching, and exploring until we had to make a move to clean up a little. Covered with cooling semen from head to toe, a washing was needed very badly. I sat up, wiggled my ass back until I was resting on a mound of pillows, then let my eyes close as Cooper talked to himself steadily in the bathroom. The sound of his voice was so soothing to me. Something about the timbre and cadence. I dropped off instantly.

What seemed like a second later, someone was swiping at my leg, dragging a wet cloth down my inner thigh, the cloth slowly moving over my stump.

I flung my hand out, grabbed Cooper's thin wrist, and stopped him cold. His eyes darted from my leg to my face, eyes wide.

"Don't touch it," I barked, half-asleep, but fully disgusted.

"Why?" I stared at him as if he had gone fully around the bend. "It's just a part of your body. Just like your face." He touched my cheek with a warm, damp hand. "Or your shoulder." He patted the scar on my shoulder. "Or your chest." His palm came to rest on my pectoral right over my thumping heart. "Or your cock." He took my limp dick in his hand. "I don't find it off-putting. I think it's a part of you. Nothing more and nothing less. Will you let me wash you off?"

I stared into those dark, soulful eyes of his. There was no trace of artifice or repulsion. He sat there, naked, exposed, just as I was, waiting in that patient way he had. It was like he knew I could catch up if given enough time.

"People turn away from me. From this." I slapped at my scarred thigh.

"I'm not turning away." Water dripped from the cloth to the bed. His demeanor never changed. "Will you let me wash you off?"

My fingers slowly uncurled from around his wrist. He smiled at me, his gaze filled with praise and affection. With infinite care he soaped, then wiped, my stump, his chit-chat about carnival rides that opened portals to hell barely registering. The skin he was touching tingled with life as if reacting in joy to the human touch that was related to something medical.

Then he did something that I never expected another human being to do. He bent down to kiss my stump. I stared for several long seconds and then I cried. Just broke right down like a damn baby and wept. Cooper tossed the washcloth to the floor, clambered onto my lap, and securely wiggled into my heart forever. He led my cheek to his shoulder, stroking my head as I slobbered all over him. When the worst of it was done, I snuffled loudly, embarrassed beyond belief. What the hell had happened to me? What kind of hockey player cried over a simple kiss?

"I think we should have a wager."

That got my attention. I swiped at my eyes with the tips of my fingers, my head coming slowly up and off his shoulder. By now, I was getting accustomed to his rapid leaps from one topic to another. Sometimes even during a dramatic moment such as we'd just had.

"Uhm… okay?"

"Here it is." He moved around, his legs straddling my thighs, his hair a total mess, his eyes bright and clever. "If you work super hard and get into your new prothesis by Christmas Day, I'll go to Canada with you to see your home."

"And the Northern Lights?"

"Well, obviously."

"Sure, yes, obviously. Okay, yes, I like that wager. One month from now, you will see me in that fancy space leg of yours. Then, I will show you the glory of Canada in winter."

"Deal." He held out his hand. I clasped it and shook. Then I flipped us over, him going to his back with a squeak. I removed his glasses—it was doubtful he could see a thing through the filthy lenses—and placed them on the nightstand. "Oh my. Are you going to have sex with me again?"

"If you wish me to sex you up, then yes. I adore you, Cooper."

His mouth parted just a little. "I adore you too, Moral." That made me happy. "Can we get sexed up now?"

"Impatient man." I chuckled before lowering my mouth to his.

We ate our cheesecake for breakfast.

THIRTEEN

Cooper

FIFTY STEPS HAD BECOME TWO HUNDRED, WHICH HAD moved onto five hundred, and this morning, Moral had passed one thousand steady steps on the treadmill. Today, was the first day he was able to walk without holding onto the bars. They were there if he needed to grab them, but he stubbornly refused, balancing his walk with his arms outright like a tightrope walker. That had been my idea.

The blade was still not ready to be an option for use in any real way, but only a week had passed, and Moral was pushing through everything like the true hero he was. The base readings I had gave us a graph of achievement, and everything was on the up.

Including my sex life.

Well, my frotting, licking, sucking, kissing life anyway. And that is all sex as far as I am concerned. The rest of it was a learning process, and we were taking it slow.

Frustratingly slow.

Still, that gave me more time to learn about Moral. Like

the fact he loved dogs of all kinds and preferred my sofa to my bed. He loved to stare out at the city from the roof, and he really loved kissing me. We'd gotten used to spending some of our downtime curled up on the sofa, me on his lap -- because hell, I wasn't turning that down -- watching reruns of old shows. He wanted me to watch *The Big Bang Theory,* maybe because my name was Cooper and he thought that I'd get a kick out of string theory, or the comedy, I wasn't sure.

I lasted three episodes, but halfway through episode four, turned off the television.

"Nope," I said without hesitation.

"What?" Moral tilted my chin to look up at him.

"I get the bit about the need to be surrounded by people who love unconditionally and accept Sheldon as he is and support him. I love that he's not seen as crazy, or out there, and I've watched videos where the character talks about string theory. He's in a safe space where people might smile and pat him on the head, but they don't ignore him. It's not like he has low self-esteem or even cares what people think of him."

"Okay…"

I probably wasn't making any sense at all. "Sheldon can do brilliant work and have all the respect from society, without the need for good social skills, and he can control his reactions to triggers. It's like this perfect sunshine life, and even his meltdowns are shown to be more about anger than reacting to the chaos in his head."

"Do you have chaos right now?"

I closed my eyes, and I could hear the reassuring tick of the big clock and the steadiness of Moral's breathing. I was warm and safe wrapped in his arms, not to mention he smelled really good. His sweater was clearly an old one, worn and soft against my fingers, and the room was lit only by some small lamps and the television.

"No. Not right now."

"We don't have to watch it at all. I don't know what I was thinking. I'm sorry if I've offended you."

"God, no! You haven't offended me, it's just... losing my parents, growing up so fast in academia, not being diagnosed and not entirely sure of my place in things, I would have killed to have friends like Sheldon had -- that laughed with me and not at me."

"Oh, Cooper, I'm sorry."

"Don't be. I'm with you now, and that is my new happy place." Did I sound too needy—it wasn't often that I wanted people around me, let alone friends. I wasn't happy being labeled as eccentric, brilliant, weird, and odd by people I got close to, but they weren't entirely wrong about what they said.

I just wanted them to love me for being me.

I wanted Moral to hold me like this for the rest of my life, where I felt safe...

... and loved.

"There will always be room on my lap for you," Moral whispered, pulling me into a close embrace.

I rested my head against his broad chest, hearing the steady thuds of his heart, knowing how close he'd been to dying, and thanking science and emergency medicine for keeping him alive.

"We'll find something else to watch," Moral said and

laced his hand with mine. "What are your feelings about nature programs?"

"As long as none of the animals die, it's all good. I'm not good at the whole circle of life thing. I once saw this show about meerkats. The camera guys named the pups Ren and Stumpy, not Stimpy, but Stumpy because he had a deformed leg."

"A bit like me then," Moral deadpanned. "You can call me Stumpy now."

"No! Because Stumpy died, and Ren was taken by an eagle, and it traumatized me. This is why I can't watch nature shows."

"Umm... true crime?"

"Nope."

"So the Discovery Channel is out, the true crime channel is out. We could just sit here and talk."

"I do have a..." Suddenly, I felt embarrassed because not everyone understood my love for movies with this plotline, but this was Moral, and he hadn't laughed at me so far. "I have a subscription to the Hallmark Channel."

"Romance movies?"

Well, he didn't seem to be weirded out—if anything, he sounded intrigued.

"There's this one where the hero is trying to save his parents' farm, and... would you like to see it?"

"I'd love to."

I flicked the television back on and scrolled to the channel, then feeling mortified—but in a good way—to the list of my saved favorites. What did it say about a man who watched romance?

"Wait, is that a hockey movie?"

"Well, the hero is an ex-hockey player who messed up on ice doing something he shouldn't have, so he has an image problem. He goes back to his hometown in Vermont and saves the town's Christmas tree lighting by taking up figure skating with the heroine who hates him for leaving town in the first place."

"Ahhh, cool. Let's watch that one then."

He shuffled a little to get comfortable, and I pressed play as he gathered me close and held me tight.

Maybe he fell asleep first, or maybe I did.

Either way, when I woke up, it was morning, and I'd never slept more peacefully than when being held by Moral.

THE BOARD MEETING WAS BORING, AND THE POT OF jellybeans had a disproportionate amount of red beans, which meant the rainbow I laid out on my notes looked all kinds of wrong. I ate the three extra that were messing things up, but the green option was still woefully underrepresented.

"I need extra of the green jellybeans," I whispered to Brianna who sat at my side taking notes. She knew I didn't pay much attention in these meetings and relied on her summarizing the latest thing the board wanted me to do.

She reached across two men in suits and yanked their pot toward her, and I could see immediately that, somehow, they'd gotten way more green jellybeans than I had. I made a mental note to suggest equality of jellybean flavor, then tuned back into what they were saying.

"… costed the treadmill roll out."

"Costed?" I said immediately. "It shouldn't cost anyone. This is something I want to make available for free." I caught Uncle Jeremiah's pinched expression, and clearly, I'd tuned out at the wrong moment.

"As I told them," Uncle Jeremiah muttered.

The one thing I didn't like about having invented Coopersil was that I was now an accidental multi-millionaire with a board and trustees, who had to, not only attend these meetings, but also agree with what they said. Mostly, it was about stock options and public perception, and mostly I could ignore that, but the treadmill I'd worked on for Moral wasn't something I wanted to make money on.

"Roll out should begin as soon as possible, with no cost attached, to all therapy-based locations dealing with amputees, and that's the end of it," I stated unequivocally. All eyes turned to me, but I channeled my inner strength and tilted my head, refusing to budge. It didn't matter that my stomach was in knots—I wanted this done.

God knows what they would say when I suggested the work I was doing on the blade was also going to be made available to all. I get that I have to answer to the board— but maybe I should think about buying back stock and not having a board at all? Fuck knows, but right now, I could sense that people were pissed at me, and I didn't like it. Without Coopersil, none of the suits at the table would even be here, and I still owned sixty percent of my company.

"Cooper, I don't know how to word this delicately."

Albert Hannington, seventy-six, former banker and serial board sitter, spoke up.

"I don't need you to word anything delicately." I was confused. Why did people always say this to me?

Brianna patted my knee, and I knew it could either mean she had my back, or that she wanted me to calm down. Right now, I was in fight mode. Moral had told me he felt lucky that he had the opportunity to try the blade and to work with my team, and he mentioned that he wished other people could get the intense focus he was getting.

He told me he was humbled by it all.

"The treadmill is free to any therapy center that needs it. I'll fund it from my own money."

"You're failing to understand that it's not merely about money," Hannington said and glanced around the table. I couldn't read his expression, but his tone was supercilious, and I bet everyone else at the table felt the same. Well, apart from Brianna and Uncle Jeremiah, who would never let money get in the way of helping people.

"And you're failing to understand that I know it's *entirely* about the money, and when it comes down to it, this is my company."

Everyone was deadly silent, and I casually picked up a scarlet jellybean and ate it slowly. Inside, my stomach was in knots, and my chest was tight with temper. The room was too warm, my suit jacket didn't sit quite right, and the whiteboard was at a weird angle. Someone had written the date on it and the words were jumbled, and Brianna patting my leg was too much. I stood up sharply when fight mode turned to flight.

"I need to go," I announced.

"It's not finished yet—"

"We'll reconvene." I looked down at Brianna who frowned up at me. A hundred kinds of concerned. "Brianna, can you…"

"Yes, sir."

I left the room after exchanging a nod with Uncle Jeremiah, and with Tony at my side, I headed for the fire stairs.

"You okay, boss?" he asked after we'd climbed three flights at top speed and I had to stop to breathe. Tony, damn him, didn't even look winded. I slid down the wall and parked my ass on the concrete step, drawing my knees up to me, then closed my eyes and rocked slowly. Feeling the messy itch of confusion in my head, it was too much for me to handle right now. I breathed slowly, but my thoughts and feelings were a scratchy knot of turmoil, and I buried my face against my knees. I don't know how long we sat there, but when I opened my eyes again, Tony was sitting next to me, scrolling through his phone as if this was a scheduled stop on the stairs. He was looking at photos of a girl and a boy—the girl had long blond curls and the boy was a miniature of his dad.

"Are those your children?"

Tony didn't react to my question by immediately asking me if I was okay. He merely tilted the phone so I could see.

"Abby and Bradley" he said with great pride and scrolled through some more until he stopped at a photo of a beautiful woman with the same blond hair as his daughter. "And this is Izzy; Isobel actually."

"She's beautiful," I offered. "I can't wait to meet her and the kids. You know, I said they could come up and use the pool. And it's been a while now, and I'm okay with it."

Tony side-eyed me, and I knew what he was thinking —it probably hadn't been long enough for me to come to terms with more people in my space. But Moral was up there with me more often than not, working on stretching or having lunch with me or watching romance movies that all had the same plot. I'd let him in, and maybe I could let others in.

Just a few.

"Tomorrow," I said with certainty. "It's Saturday, are you free to bring them up, and we'll have a pool party."

"Okay, I'll check with Izzy."

"Good, that's awesome." We sat in silence for a moment longer. "Can I ask you a question?"

"You don't usually ask me if you can ask me," Tony said, and he was smiling, so that was okay.

"This is important."

"Go on then."

"When did you know you were in love with Izzy?"

His smile widened. "The moment she called me on my shit and told me that just because I was military, she wasn't going to fall in bed with me."

"Oh." I picked at a loose thread on my shirt. "Is it easy?"

"What?"

"Being in love?"

"It was easy to fall in love, and it's easy to love Izzy every day, so I guess, yeah?"

"I think I'm falling in love with Moral, but I'm not sure when it happened or why."

Tony shrugged, closed his phone and slipped it into his pocket. "Sometimes you don't have to know the why, just that it's happened."

"We haven't had sex yet," I blurted. "I mean, we have great orgasms together, but some people only define sex as... y'know." I winced at my lack of filter and the fact that I had made a loop with one hand and was pushing a finger into the loop.

"It'll happen if you want it to."

"Yeah."

We finished the journey to Moral's floor in silence, and when I walked into the huge gym, Moral was there with his friend Marquis and another guy, who was shorter, wearing a jersey with the name ROWE on the back. Now wasn't the time to talk about sex with Moral, and I already regretted talking to Tony, but for now, I wanted to be with Moral, and if that included his friends, then I could handle that.

Right?

FOURTEEN

Moral

I COULDN'T STOP THE SMILE THAT OVERTOOK MY FACE from seeing Cooper. There was no way to stop it, and even if I could have, I wouldn't have. Marquis, who was spotting Austin now, watched as I rose with ease from the shoulder press machine, placed my weight evenly on my good leg and my old prosthesis, and grabbed the new cane Cooper's foundation had supplied. It was a cool, manly thing, all black with some kick-ass skulls and deep red roses on it. Reminded me of a heavy metal album. I'd loved it at first sight and kissed Cooper for about an hour after he had presented it to me a few days ago.

I'd made some considerable progress over the past few weeks. Real progress. Like the kind that was showing me that I would have a fulfilling life even if I was an amputee. Even being able to acknowledge that terminology was a huge step forward, according to my therapist. Like the kind that had me wearing shorts to workout, allowing my friends to see my fake leg. I'd not worked up to letting them see my stump. Maybe someday. Not yet. But hey! Shorts and a prosthetic was a big step for a man with only one foot.

"Hey," I called as Cooper and Tony lingered in the doorway of the gym. Tony looking like the head of the Secret Service sans the dark shades, and Cooper looking slightly uncomfortable. I made my way to them, taking care to ensure that I placed my weight evenly on the cane and the prosthetic at the same time. Then, it was as simple as weight on my intact limb, weight on the cane and prosthetic, repeat, until you got where you were going. It took me a little while to cross the room. Speedy, I was not, but I got there, grinning like a madman when I was standing in front of Cooper. His tender smile gave me the shivers. Maybe it was because I was sweaty, but I didn't think so. There was a lot of emotion in those pretty brown eyes of his. "I wasn't expecting you until our swim later today. I invited a couple of the guys over to workout with me. That okay?"

Cooper nodded, his teeth worrying his bottom lip for a moment, the soft smile gone. I knew he wasn't always able to deal with new people and/or disruptions to his routine. So I gave him a small peck on the cheek. That helped erase some of the disquiet, as did just letting him have space and time.

"Yes, of course, this is your floor. Oh, there's Penelope." He rushed over to the dog napping in the meager November sunlight pouring through the windows. He'd taken to my loveable old gal quickly, and now always had dog treats in his pockets. Sometimes, so many his pockets bulged. Penelope tended to follow him around, hoovering up the treats that fell from his overflowing pockets. I loved that she loved him so much. He was so easy to love.

"He here for a reason?" I asked Tony as Cooper fussed over the dog.

"Tough board meeting. He seems to come to you now when he's upset or anxious."

"Ah." I glanced back at my dog and my lover lying in the sun. Penelope on her belly chomping on a biscuit and Cooper mimicking her. Thankfully, he wasn't chewing on a dog treat. He was plucking jellybeans from a baggie he'd pulled from his back pocket. Have jellybeans will travel. I looked from Cooper to Tony. "Is that a problem? Him coming here when he's feeling anxious?"

"Not at all, as long as you don't end up upsetting him. He cares for you a lot. Don't hurt him." With that, he stepped out of the room, closing the door quietly. I knew he would be right outside. Guess he trusted me and my friends with his boss. Which was good. No one here would ever hurt Cooper. If anyone tried, I'd beat them to a pulp.

Okay. So, I turned around carefully, leaning on my good leg, and met Marquis's curious look.

"Umm… some help here?!" Austin squeaked, his arms trembling as he struggled with the weights he was lifting. Marquis was quick to grab the barbell and guide it into place. Austin lay there, panting, his face red. "Man, pay attention."

"Sorry, I was just… thought I saw something," Marquis replied, tossing a towel to Austin as the young man shakily sat up. "Guess we should get moving. We need to nap before the game tonight. You coming, Dunny?"

"I, umm…" I shrugged. It was petty of me to not go cheer on my team. I knew that. But I just wasn't ready. The fans all looked at me with pity. The TV announcers all commended me for my bravery and courage. It was just too much. I missed hockey so badly it was an ache that rivaled the worst tooth pain. Someday, when I could skate, when I was whole again, I'd go to a Rebels game. Maybe. If only I could find a way to still be involved in the game as I was now. Seeing the sympathy in everyone's eyes only reminded me of what I had lost. I needed to get into the game the way I was now. The new Dunny needed a new way to do hockey…

"It's cool. Watch us on TV, though. We're playing the Railers." Marquis padded over to give my neck a squeeze while Austin mopped his face dry. "Also," he whispered, "we are going to talk about the kissing the cute scientist thing my eyeballs just witnessed."

"Right. We'll talk. Now, take Rowe home so he can get a nap and some carbs." I stood by the door, smiling as my buddies filed out, leaving me and Cooper alone. Well, aside from Penelope, and she wasn't going to tell anyone what we got up to. I limped my way to the corner, resting on my cane, the sun hitting the side of my face, and leaned on the wall, easing my ass down until I was seated on the floor. Probably not the smartest thing I had ever done, since getting up from the floor was a damn battle at times. Still, here I was, on the same level as Cooper and my pooch.

"Where is your family?" Cooper asked, moving to lie

on his side, his hand holding his head, his yellow framed glasses slightly crooked on his face. "Will they walk in on us if we decide to cuddle?"

A little fizzy jolt of desire raced to my balls. Cuddling with this man was not always just hugging. More and more of late cuddling could mean all kinds of things, from a simple kiss to frottage to hand and/or blow jobs.

"They're at the Citizens Bank Opera House, seeing a matinee performance of *Hairspray*." I shifted my hips a little to try to hide the erection tenting the front of my basketball shorts.

"Oh okay, good." He pushed up to his knees, then scooted over to me, taking a moment to grab a towel from the pile beside the small table holding bottles of water. "I'd like to try something out."

He handed me the towel. "Okay. What are we trying out?"

"I think it's time we have sex." He removed his shirt and placed it on the floor. I looked around the gym, trying to sort out the ten thousand conflicting ideas whirling around inside my head.

"You want to have sex here in the gym?" I finally asked, my sight flying to him as he unbuckled his belt. "It smells like sweaty men in here."

"Yes, not a wholly unappealing aroma. You have some wonderfully intoxicating pheromones. I've picked them up before when you exercise." He moved to lie on his back to remove his pants. My dick was all gung-ho with this idea. I had always enjoyed doing it in places other than a bed. I just wasn't sure Cooper wanted our first time to be here in a gym with a sleepy basset hound snoring in the corner. He arched up, removed his pants and briefs, and then sat up to tug off his socks. He took a moment to line up his clothing. Once he was naked and had his clothes where he liked them, he fished his wallet out of his pocket. Four little red dog treats fell out, but Penelope was back in her bed snuffling after a dream bunny. He took a condom and a packet of lube out of his wallet, nodded to himself, and placed his slacks to the tiled floor. His cock was rigid, the head flushed dark red, the slit weeping. Okay, so he did want our first time to be here in the gym. Obviously, he was into it, or he wouldn't be sporting such a massive hard-on. "Also, this seems the most likely place to have an erotic rendezvous."

"What about the bedroom? Oh, okay, yeah, this is good." He climbed into my lap, placing his bare ass on my thighs, and linked his arms around my neck. His mouth settled over mine, his fingers toying with the hairs on the back of my neck.

"Mm, you taste like orange juice," he purred, licking into my mouth for another taste while moving his pert ass back and forth over my dick. "You should always drink lots of orange juice. The vitamin C will help aid healing. Also, it keeps you from getting scurvy."

"Good to know if I ever want to be a pirate. Cooper, I… shit, move to the left, yeah good. Okay. Nice. Nice. Ride me like that." He rocked back and forth and eased my wet Rebels tee over my head, his eyes hot behind his smudged glasses. I cradled his ass, kneading the bare orbs, pressing in slightly to add more friction to the bump and grind. His kisses roamed over my face, dropping small touches to my cheeks, eyes, and the scar that so many people shied away from. A shudder rolled through me, my breath hitching as he nipped at my lower lip just as his hand slid between us. His fingers continued going down my damp belly into my shorts. He had a strong grip for such a small man. I bucked up into his fist, sucking on his tongue now, fully into having sex on the floor of the gym. I'd make love to this man anywhere and at any time my desire for him was so strong.

"Let's take these off," he breathlessly suggested, releasing my cock to pull frantically at the elastic band of my shorts. "Do you want to take off your prosthetic?" I nodded, grunted something in French, and used my good leg to hoist my ass up off the floor. He slid off my lap, kneeling beside me to remove my clunky old prosthetic, then my shorts, briefs, sneaker, and sock. He took the time to line them all up in a row to our left before bending down to kiss the head of my cock. His tongue slid over the head peeking out of my foreskin. My cock was oozing precum.

"You okay?" I asked when he licked his lips. The look I got was incendiary. Pupils blown, hair tousled, lips shiny. He was every wet dream I'd ever had come to life. And he was mine.

"Of course. I'm not repelled by casual contact with people's microbiomes, at least I don't think so." He took another lap, then another, then he took my cock into his mouth. My head hit the wall with a thud as I squeezed my eyes shut and tried to recall Guy Lafleur's stats. Anything to not blow my nut before we even got started. "Mm, yes, I like your taste. Can I lick more of you?"

"God yes," I panted, my fingers squeaking over the

flooring as he moved from my cock to my inner thigh. My eyes flew open when his lips moved lower still on my right leg. "Cooper, no, I, no…" He stopped instantly and sat up to study me as he did when he was working something out. "You don't want to kiss that."

"But I do. I like the taste of you. This is a part of you, like your elbow or your anus. If I wanted to tongue your anus, would you object?" I opened my mouth, then shut it. He leaned in to kiss me on the mouth. "I'd like to kiss you all over, but I won't if you don't want me to."

"Sure, yeah, okay, hold on. Just…" I gasped as he shifted a leg over me, his ass sliding sensually over my cock. "Cooper, I'm sorry for stopping you. It's just… it's not pretty."

"Everything about you is pretty." He took my face in his hands and kissed into my mouth, smearing the taste of myself all over my tongue. "I like this so much. Will you work me open with your fingers? I've been studying anal sex, and I think I'm going to like it. I enjoy your fingers inside me when you suck my dick. Prostate play is so enjoyable. I think I'm very much into anal play, but not so much placing my mouth on your butt. Even though I did offer before, that was merely to make a point that I love every part of your body. Even your stump. I'm a body lover. Sometimes, I think of my sexuality as more than a biological urge and—"

"Cooper, please stop talking and hand me the lube." I was this close to coming. His eyes went wide, his cheeks flushed, and he quickly handed me the packet of lube. I ripped it open with my teeth and smeared it over my fingers. He went up to his knees with a soft little mewl. I captured a nipple and sucked it as I slid my fingers down the crack of his ass. He placed his hands on my shoulders as I nibbled his nipple and played with his hole. His breathing picked up as I worked a finger into him.

"That's good. Mm, so good. Yes, wiggle it. Oh!" His fingers bit into my flesh. I stroked that spot more, lightly at first, then with more pressure. He began riding my finger, and I added a second. His head rolled back and forth, his glasses sliding off to land beside us. I flicked them away so not to break them. I released his nipple and moved to the other, all the while massaging his prostate, pulling soft, hot growls and whimpers from him.

"You want me now? You're ready," I huffed, leaving my fingers buried inside him until I heard otherwise.

"Yes, yes, I want you inside me." He looked down at me, his brow slick with sweat, his lips swollen from kissing. I eased my fingers out and fumbled with the condom as he sucked on my neck, his hands knotted in my hair. How I ever got the damn rubber on I have no clue, but I did. Using my slick fingers, I smeared a little lube over my cock.

"Sit still now, baby. Up on your knees… shit. Yeah, now easy. Go slow." I held tightly to the base of my cock, the head now resting at his opening. "Don't sit down too fast. Go slow. Easy, baby, easy."

He eased downward, incrementally, his body stretching around me, gripping me, hot and slick and… *fuck*. He felt so good. I released my prick to hold him close. His body was tense, his brow coming down to rest on mine.

"You're huge," he panted, his fingernails scoring my shoulders, his sweat slipping down his back to where my fingers rested on his lumbar. "I like it. The burn... the feel of your big dick deep inside me. Oh, Moral, I like it so much. I love it. We... ugh, oh heck, we must do this again!"

"We'll do this as often as you want, baby." I gently tasted his lips. He settled down on my lap, my cock fully seated, catching his breath as I peppered his jaw with tiny kisses. "Any time you want me you just say so. I love this—"

"Love this... too." He flicked his hips. We both hissed in pleasure. "Oh! Oh! That's amazing. So amazing." He rocked up, then sat down. Something inside my brain kind of disconnected when he began riding me in earnest. Slow at first. The pace began to pick up as his body and mine demanded more. I took his cock in hand and gave it a stroke. That was all it took. Cooper fell into me, his body convulsing, warm cum coating my fingers, belly, and chest. His ragged breath and the soft moans of his orgasm did me in. My balls tightened. My cock exploded, filling the condom with pulse after pulse of pure pleasure. I held him close, my nose in his chest, breathing in all the delicious smells of sweat, sex, and Cooper.

We sat there, the floor not cold under my ass now, gasping as we fought to catch our breath, his body growing pliant as we drifted back to Earth.

"I like sex with you," he whispered, his forehead still touching mine. My eyes flickered open. His dark gaze locked with mine. Yeah, he did like sex. That was obvious. "Actually, I think I love you. I have all the symptoms. Every time I see you, I feel euphoric and emotionally unstable, yet giddy about it. My thoughts are always being intruded upon with musings of you. Our interests are aligned. I feel possessive of you and your time. My cheeks flush, my palms get sweaty, and my pulse rises whenever you're near me. Do you feel the same, Moral?"

"I do. Yeah, I got all of them symptoms and more."

"Good. Good. We're both in love. That's wonderful. Uncle Jeremiah and Brianna will be happy. I bet they'll buy us a cake."

That one made me chuckle. "Do they make cakes for people in love?"

"Well surely. They make cards for them." He looked at me as if cakes for lovers were a common thing. Hell, who knew, maybe they were. Maybe they had them in the grocery store in the frozen cake aisle. "And they make songs about being in love. Yes, they must have cakes. I hope they have cake. We should have a cake. With our names and the date and time we had sex written on it with yellow frosting. Do you like chocolate cake? I do. If not, we can get a half vanilla and half... why are you laughing?"

"No reason, baby, you just make me happy."

A smile tugged at the corners of his mouth. "You make me happy too."

"As happy as chocolate cake with yellow lettering?" I gave his bare backside a squeeze. He snorted in amusement and moved up and off me with a little sigh before he was curled into me, his cheek on my scarred shoulder. We'd have to clean up and get dressed soon. But not just yet...

"Yes, even more than cake. So much more than cake," he admitted as he melted into my embrace.

"Yeah, same here, baby. I love you more than cake."

Talk about a glorious and unexpected gift. Maybe God was looking down on me after all and decided that, since he took my leg, he'd give me a soul mate. Holding Cooper close to me as the sun warmed us, I had to think that maybe that was a fair deal the almighty had given me.

FIFTEEN

Cooper

BEING IN LOVE WAS WONDERFUL, AND AT THE SAME TIME, frightening. The awesome part was that everything in my life seemed to glow with the magic of it all. The frightening part was navigating love at the same time as having a professional relationship with Moral, not to mention my fears that I wasn't doing the whole being together thing right. Neither of these things were conducive to me sitting in the emergency board meeting called to replace the one I'd walked out of. Love made me doodle ladybugs to form heart shapes, worries about what was next for Moral and how I could do my best for him making me frown, but it was the boredom of sitting here that had me switching off.

Brianna nudged me, and I glanced at her. "The delivery of the treadmills has been authorized."

Can I go now?

She must have read my silent plea because she gave a subtle shake of her head, and I grimaced because all I wanted to do was go back to my lab and keep working on what I was creating.

We'd worked on the additions to the basic prosthetic that we'd created for walking—the one that had settled so well for Moral—and now had ones with shoe attachments, which proved to be yet another mountain that he had to climb. But the pièce de résistance, the pinnacle of what I was working on, was still a secret, even from Moral, let alone Brianna and Uncle Jeremiah. Tony was the only one who knew and was tasked with keeping everyone away from my lab, on pain of death—and yes, that is what I made him swear to.

The final tranche of data for the first prosthetic—the walking one— was waiting on my server, and at first glance, looked promising. The swelling was minimal and managed, the ease of fit and the calibration of the addition was perfect, and most of all, it was Moral approved. I worried that the flex in the metal was causing an imbalance, and that this could lead to issues in people less athletic than Moral. I'd already noticed that he was favoring his left leg, which suggested that maybe the metal was flexing too much, and I really needed to—

"—reinforcement?"

Brianna patted my knee—harder this time—and cleared her throat. This meant I'd missed something important, zoned out into what she and my uncle fondly called Coop-Space.

"Apologies," I said, glancing around the table, not entirely sure who had even been speaking. "For clarity, could you repeat the question?" This was one of the tricks that Brianna had taught me, and it meant I didn't look as if

I was sitting here bored and not listening. She was very good at giving me coping strategies, so no one realized I *was* bored and that I *wasn't listening*.

Albert Hannington—I should have known—raised an eyebrow at me, which could mean anything at all, and then he checked his notes.

"The basement reinforcing costs are exceeding the budget and the building of an ice rink," his eyebrow raised even higher, "has become something of a money pit."

I paused for a moment, considering my response in that careful way Brianna suggested I do. She'd also told me to meet people's gazes, but right now I focused on his eyebrows and thinning hair, which was a lot less intimidating.

"The rink will be completed by tomorrow, on schedule, and to do this, we've engaged extra staff—a small price to pay for efficiency."

"The second part of my detailed enquiry was the future use of the rink."

"What future use?" I checked the cheat notes Brianna had created for me. Nope. Nothing about future use.

"Will you be opening the rink to the public? Is it a capital expenditure that we can write off against R&D? Is it a gift for your... let's say, patient, in which case this is a personal cost?"

It seemed to me that everyone in the room held their collective breaths, including me, because the way he'd just said it sounded wrong. I didn't get what he was trying to say, and I bet he was implying something that was going right over my head.

"The staff can use it," I offered, and I swear Albert

Hannington smirked. What was going on here? I was so confused.

"And the cost of running the refrigeration systems, and umm…" He shuffled his notes to impress that he'd researched this, and Brianna, sitting next to me, cursed under her breath and called Albert a name I'd never heard her use. "… a mini-Zamboni, whose delivery entailed tunneling from the level above. Not to mention a snack area?"

"It will be realistic," I said with enthusiasm, "and however we need to pay for it, we pay for it. I want Moral —Mr. Dunkirk—to have the most authentic experience possible so that the prosthetics are—"

"We're aware of your personal relationship with Mr. Dunkirk," Albert said, and a couple of the board members cautiously nodded.

"So?" *Okay, maybe that was rude?*

"Our concern is that shareholders may see the expense as—"

"I'll pay for this personally," I interrupted, but all Albert did was sigh.

That wasn't right. I think he was disrespecting me? Was he? Next to me, Brianna was bristling, and her hand tightened on my leg for a moment, probably warning me not to react to whatever was going on. Hell, I wished I knew what was going on.

"That's not entirely the point," Albert began, exchanging glances with the same board members who'd been doing their best nodding dog impressions earlier. "You probably don't understand."

"I *probably* don't understand what, exactly?" I was bemused and not sure where this was going.

"Shareholders will be concerned that money is being frittered away on wasteful projects just because you are *seeing* someone."

"Seeing what? Who?"

Albert rolled his eyes. *He rolled his eyes!*

"We don't want to suggest anything untoward, but you have a responsibility to your shareholders, and we're concerned your mental health issues and your personal relationships are corrupting your decision-making process and costing money."

That sounded rehearsed. "I'm not following?" My mental health issues, I didn't have... wait. "You mean the shareholders are concerned *my autism* might cost them money? When it was due to *my autism* that I was able to create Coopersil in the first place?"

"Well, no one mentioned the A-word," Albert began, but I cut him off by standing up and letting my chair bang against the bank of glass windows with a view over the park.

He stopped talking. He *so* did not go there. "And by seeing someone, do you mean the fact I'm having sex with Moral?" Someone gasped, and I knew instantly maybe I shouldn't have shared that at all, but Brianna was smiling. "I did what the board asked. I'm working on a project I never wanted to be the public face of. Furthermore, Mr. Dunkirk is our patient, and what he is working on with us will bring a lot of money into CAHTech, which is, after all, the bottom line. Unless, of course, I hand all my research over to anyone who wants it for the good of the world?" They didn't know I intended to do that, anyway.

"Now, look, I didn't mean to imply—"

I was exasperated because I'd heard this all before, people willing to take and use what I made, but then judging me for the man I was, all because of how my brain worked. Not Moral—he found me funny and cute and sexy, and he loved my brain. I wish he was here now.

"You meant to make me look stupid by bring up my relationship with Moral Dunkirk. And it's not the A-word; it's autism, got it?"

"I meant no disrespect—"

"You meant disrespect! You want me to look stupid, and I can tell you now that I might look at things differently than you, but I am far from stupid." Then it hit me. "Brianna, do our board member contracts contain termination provisions?"

They all paled, and Brianna was up and next to me immediately, realizing that this was yet another tedious meeting I was walking away from.

"I believe they do," she confirmed.

"And as the majority shareholder, currently holding sixty percent of *my* company that is only here because of what *I* created, do I have the right to build an ice rink in the basement of a building that *my* company paid for in order to create a product that will build on *our* reputation?"

"Yes."

"And also, do I have the right to a private life?"

"You have the right to do whatever you want, sir." Brianna followed me to the door, along with Tony. I opened it to let them go through first. As soon as it was shut, and there was a barrier between us and them, I felt the adrenaline leave my body.

And there was only one place I wanted to go.

Or rather, one person I wanted to see.

And after a quick stop in my development lab, it was Moral I hunted down.

We finally found him down in the basement, sitting on one of the chairs on the outside of the new rink. The space was cold, and I wished I'd thought to bring a jacket, but Moral was sitting there, arms crossed over his chest, staring out at the new ice. He didn't notice me and Tony approaching until the last minute. When he realized it was me, he smiled so hard that I wanted to kiss him there and then, but I didn't know who was watching, with several people milling around the basement doing this and that.

"Hi," he said and moved in his chair to face me. He was wearing the first blade, the one that I'd designed for walking, and he had the shoe attached, which I could see below the hem of his jeans. Tony left my side prowling around the edge of the rink, and I took a seat next to Moral, setting the large box I carried to one side.

"Hi."

"Good meeting?" Moral asked. He knew where I'd been and had seen firsthand how frustrated I'd been this morning that I even had to go. I was so close to finishing the surprise I had for him, and I didn't want delays of having to show my face at meaningless meetings, particularly ones where I felt like I was in trouble most of the time.

"Yeah, mostly. I mean, I think I fired someone, but I'm not sure."

"You think?"

"Yeah, he was making all these suggestions about you, me, and the rink overspend, and so I got myself all stressed out."

"And you fired him?"

"No, but I threatened him. I think."

"I'm sure he deserved it."

"He absolutely did. Anyway, there's something I want to give you. Something I've done, and I don't want to overstep, but I genuinely hope right now is the time, that this would be good to take the next step, or skate, so to speak. I don't think you'll be upset, but I want you to know that I've done this with the best of intentions—"

"Did you kill someone?"

"What? No."

"Shame, because Marquis is on my hit list," Moral deadpanned.

"No, this could be something worse if you don't like it, and I tried to—"

He leaned over and pressed a finger to my lips. "I love everything you do. Everything."

I blinked at him, seeing the utter conviction in his beautiful eyes, and I swear I was about to combust right in front of him. He was giving me unconditional and unwavering acceptance, and I loved him for that.

Flustered, I yanked the box over, leaning off balance, and nearly falling off the chair until Moral caught me and chuckled as he did so.

"Whoa," he said and held me until I wasn't about to hit the ground.

"This is for you," I said and gently passed the heavy

box to him, which he took as if it weighed nothing. "Please don't be angry with me."

Everything I felt for him was in this box—my hopes and dreams for his happiness and my certainty that he was going to be able to take back some control of what he did next.

"I could never be angry with you." He smiled and pulled at one corner of the lid, easing it off to expose the contents, and then, quickly putting the lid back on.

"Is that a…"

"It's a prototype, but it's an extension to your prosthetic."

"A skating blade?"

"Yeah. Do you like it? Did I fuck up?"

He glanced at me, and I couldn't read his expression, but he eased off the lid again, and this time, he let it fall to the ground next to him and, carefully, eased the blade out of the molded space.

"Fuck," he muttered, turning it this way and that, the bright rink lights catching the metal—a new take on Coopersil, experimental and flexible enough to skate, but rigid enough to hold him secure. "It's beautiful, sharp… wow."

"That sounds like a good wow?"

"Yes, I guess this bit…" he tilted it, "… that connects to… and this would be…" He hefted it. "It's heavy, so it might throw me at first, but… yes, it's a good wow." He placed the whole box on the seat next to him. "Thank you."

"You're welcome. I want to see you back on the ice." I waited for him to say that he was never going to skate again, or any one of the things he said about his future, but all I got was a shy smile.

"I can't wait to use it. Thank you."

Then, Moral knocked elbows with me, but it was as if he wanted more than that, and he tugged me close. I craved to be held, tight and secure, burying my face in his neck. Maybe he knew me better than I knew myself, and he clearly didn't care which one of the carefully picked engineers working on the rink might see him hugging me. Whatever it was, he put an arm over my shoulder and pulled me close, then when I was right up against his side, he half-lifted me so I was straddling his lap.

I felt Tony move in front of us, trying to block what was happening, but I didn't care, because whatever the world thought of me, Moral didn't judge me, and he didn't care what people thought—he was happy to hold me.

"I'm so pleased you're happy. It's made a shit day better."

"What happened to make it shit?" he asked as he shifted in the seat to hold me tighter. I melted against him, trusting that he would hold me and wanting nothing more.

"Things. Board nonsense. Hell, I wish we'd never taken Coopersil public. I should have kept it all, but I thought if other people were invested, we could take our developments out and away from how it started. All it ended up doing was creating people who want to stifle research because of money. It's all about money—I didn't even want all the money, I just wanted to make a difference, and get all the thoughts I had out of my head and into something practical." I sighed. "Can we just talk about something else? Tell me about your cars."

"Is that next on your list to fix for me?"

I didn't want to tell him that I was already researching the best way to adapt his cars and had been on several lengthy phone calls with a few high-end car manufacturers and motor sport teams about that very subject. Instead, I sighed to cover the pause.

Moral soothed me by pressing his hand to my back and placing a kiss on my head.

"Anyway, I have a whole garage of cars," Moral said after a moment's pause. "A '63 Red Jaguar E-type roadster, a '64 Aston Martin DB5 in silver, like James Bond's car in Goldfinger, yeah?"

"I haven't ever seen a Bond film."

He inhaled sharply and, then, chuckled. "We need to fix that. I told you about the 1990 Red Ferrari F40 before, and my everyday car is an Audi RS 6 Avant." He sighed, and I cuddled deeper. "That's not right, though is it? My everyday car *was* an Audi. Anyway, they're investments. I used to take them up to Hampden County. They have a track there, and you can push your cars as hard as you want. It used to be the highlight of my life after hockey. I kind of miss that speed, the thrill of it, hearing the engines."

"Maybe one day, you could get a car that's adapted. But not the Ferrari." I recalled him saying that.

"God no, none of those cars should be touched. It would have to be something more practical, something I can fix up. And for the other ones, I don't know whether to sell them or not—they don't deserve to be shut away and not used. I don't know. Everything feels so unsettled and unfocused right now."

I closed my eyes and inhaled the scent of him, but there was a twinge in my chest that felt a little like pain. We'd said we loved each other, and I understood the symptoms of love, but wondered if how he felt was different from how I felt? If what we had didn't settle him and make him happy, then was I seeing love the wrong way?

Maybe sex was all it was?

"But you know what?" he continued, and I screwed my eyes shut even tighter. "Being with you, holding you, loving you, that's about as perfect as things can get, and that centers me more than you could ever know. With you, I see all the possibilities, and that includes maybe skating a lap around the ice. Thank you."

I finally opened my eyes and drew back a little to kiss Moral's neck.

Love was perfect.

SIXTEEN

Moral

THERE HAVE BEEN JUST A FEW TIMES IN MY LIFE THAT I'VE cried.

When I lost my parents, obviously, that was the biggest. Or had been. Waking up after the crash, I'd wept in joy to still be alive, and then, I cried in loss over… well, just about everything.

Now, sitting at a rink inside a tower of glass and steel, with my boyfriend, I felt tears streaming down my face. He'd gifted me something that I thought might be gone to me forever. Hockey. Sniffling, I held the skating leg across my lap, my gaze unable to leave the miracle Cooper had handed to me. After I'd held him and talked nonsense about cars, he'd seemed more settled. I was ready to talk about the skate blade, only as I held it again, the emotions of everything were overwhelming—hence the tears.

"It's still a prototype. We'll streamline it, of course. Are you sad that it's so clunky looking? I can take it back to the lab and bring it back out once it's been—"

"No, no. I love it. Please, don't take it back to the lab.

Not yet." I tore my sight from the blade glistening under the lights. Damn, it looked sharp. "I'm just… a little overwhelmed. There for a long time, I thought I'd never be able to do the things that I loved. But thanks to you—"

Cooper shook his head, his slim eyebrows knitting. "It's not due to me. It's all you, Moral. I just made the tools. You're the one working your backside off to use them. You're walking with a cane now, working up to jogging, and now with this you can skate. Not at a professional level, of course, but a recreational one for sure. Perhaps, you might even be able to play on the new sled team the Rebels have formed."

"Yeah, yeah, maybe." I stroked the prosthetic and smiled at my man. "We're quite the partnership, eh?"

"We sure are."

Some scientist-type people interrupted our chat, hovering next to us.

"You want me to try it now?"

"If you want to—the team is here to support you." He gestured at the group in their lab coats.

"Okay then."

He kissed me quickly, his cheeks growing rosy, and then, he sat back to let me do my thing. With a practiced hand, I began readying myself to try out the prosthetic skate leg. I got the gel padding into place before tightening the leg down. Since I already had my liner on, I simply rolled it up to the top of my thigh, then did the same with the liner on the leg. I noted there was a small cranking knob to tighten the plastic cup that supported my leg below the knee. After giving it a few turns, not too loose or too tight, I glanced at Cooper.

"I think I'm ready to give it a try," I said. My belly was churning with trepidation. I gave it a bounce or two. Cooper laced up a skate on my good foot, but I fiddled with the laces until they were perfect.

"Take your time. I'll film your first few attempts. Let me know what works and what doesn't. I can tweak as much as you need." Cooper sat at the edge of his seat, reaching into a bag that Tony had dropped at his side, his ever-present notebooks and pens now in hand. I nodded. "Also, don't be too hard on yourself. This will take time, I'm sure."

"Right. Yeah, of course." Hand on the boards for support, I placed my skate out on the ice, inhaling the brisk clean smell of frozen water. My eyes grew dewy. I swiped the tears away. Now was not the time. Taking a deep breath, I gingerly put the blade to the ice. Several scientists gathered around Cooper, all of them jabbering at once, most with tablets and gizmos in their hands.

"Quiet, please, be quiet. We need to hear Moral's thoughts," Cooper called, his eyes never leaving me. I took a tentative step, then another, my confidence growing as I tried to locate my balance. It was not even close to how it used to feel to be on skates. Arms out, I pushed forward with my good leg.

"It's odd," I said as I brought the skate forward. "I can't use my ankle, which is weird, but I can use my knee. That helps. It feels as if I am dragging my leg. Oh, shit." I windmilled my arms to keep from falling.

"Would you like an aid? We can grab a walker," Cooper asked, shooting to his feet when I almost fell.

"No, that is… non. It is good. I'm good." I worked at

crossing the rink. Something that I would have done before in a few seconds, now took ages. Or what felt like ages. I was not the man I used to be, that was for sure, and the prosthetic felt clunky. It was not my leg. Nor would one ever be, no matter how wonderfully designed Cooper would make it. When I bumped into the boards, I gave a hoot of joy, tossing both hands into the air, then promptly falling on my ass.

Cooper and his team scurried out onto the ice, several falling over, to rescue me. I didn't need rescuing, though. I lay on the ice, panting and laughing in sheer joy.

He slid over to me, his dark eyes wide as dinner plates, before losing his balance. Down he went to his ass with a thud.

"Ouch! Oh, my butt. That's a bruise." He sat up, fixed his glasses, and rubbed his backside. "Are you okay? Are you in pain? Why are you crying again?" He reached out to gather a tear on his finger, observing it as it slid down to the ice.

"I'm just happy. I skated. *I skated!* Mostly. It was ugly and slow and stupid looking, but I did it. Cooper, mon amour, I did it." I reached up, cupped the back of his neck, and gently led his lips to mine. He kissed me back without his usual mind-melting enthusiasm. His shyness keeping the smooch a sweet expression of joy. "I have thoughts for the skate. Small things. We will work them out. Okay, I wish to go again. Someone help me up."

It took four of them to get me righted, which was funny to me. The second time, I did a little better. The third time, a little better and a little further. An hour later,

Cooper made me stop. I did, but only after I'd gone from one net to the other without falling on my ass.

"This is the second-best day of my life," I panted after I was made to leave the ice. A good call, as my stump was sore. A massage and some OTC painkillers would take care of the aching pain.

"What was the first?" Cooper enquired as he gently took the skate from my hands, his mind already calibrating. I could tell by the way his lips puckered slightly.

"Meeting you." That brought his gaze from his creation to his boyfriend.

"Oh. That's adorable. Mine too." He pecked my cheek quickly before his thoughts went back to his work. I didn't take offense. He didn't need to be tuned into me twenty-four hours a day. I had a lot to process now. Cooper would find me around dinner time, and we would cuddle and talk, maybe more, and then he would slip into my bed. Life was about as good as it could be, it seemed. The darkness was abating as I began to discover the new Moral little by little.

VALLÉE ROSE TOWER, THE ENGINE HAS STALLED. REPEAT, the engine has stalled.

Foxtrot Michael Dundee Paul, can you see the runway yet?

Vallée Rose Tower, non. I cannot see the airfield. The engine has stalled. Repeat, the engine has stalled. I am having a serious situation here.

Foxtrot Michael Dundee Paul, roger that. We have you on radar. What is your airspeed and altitude?

Vallée Rose Tower, my airspeed is one hundred five miles per hour and slowing rapidly. My altitude is three thousand feet and falling quickly.

Foxtrot Michael Dundee Paul, roger that. Pull up on the nose of the plane and bank south-southwest. We will bring you in on the farmland that should be appearing to your left. Do you see the fields yet?

Yes! Yes, Vallée Rose Tower, I do see the fields. The plane is not responsive. Repeat the plane is not responsive. I'm descending at about four hundred feet per minute.

Foxtrot Michael Dundee Paul, roger that. Remain calm. Maintain level wings and follow the woodland perimeter. Try to restart the engine. If that does not work, try throttle full forward and mixture idle cut off. Once the engine starts firing, you will have several seconds to add mixture to keep it running. Do you copy, Foxtrot Michael Dundee Paul?

Vallée Rose Tower, negative on the engine restart. Negative on the engine restart. The engine is on fire. Repeat. The engine is on fire. I see the fields now. The nose is down but the wings are level. I am going in hard. I am bracing for impact now.

Dieu sauve-moi.

"*Dieu sauve-moi!*" I bellowed, jolting upward in bed, the covers choking me. Ripping, clawing, thrashing, I freed myself from the bedding, panic sending me off the side of the bed to the floor with a crash. My arm cleared the lamp and bottles of peach seltzer from the nightstand, glass and fizzy drink cascading down over me. Glass and water. In my face. I was crashing again. The pain was coming. The agony of metal shearing off to rip into my face, my shoulder ripping from its socket, my leg pulled and wrenched and sliced open a thousand different ways. I was dying all over again.

"Moral! Oh hell!" Cooper shouted, the lights coming on as his voice began to seep into the horrors of the nightmare. I blinked, clearing the sticky drink from my eyes, my arm flopping to the carpeting where tiny slivers of broken lightbulb cut into my forearm. "Moral, are you okay?!"

"Non, stay up there," I croaked, my throat still tight with fear. "I'm good. Just some glass in my arm." The sight of him peering over the side of his massive bed, glasses haphazardly sitting on his face, his cheeks still bearing pillow creases, helped me come back from the night terrors that much faster. His eyes flared. "It's fine. Nothing but a scratch." I smiled wobblily before sitting up, my heart still pounding in my ears. When I had my back to the bed, I drew in a long breath, then let it out. My fingers found the tiny bits of glass in my arm, so I began flicking them out of my skin with my thumbnail. Anything to keep my mind focused on the here and now. "See, they come right out."

He ran his hands over my head, his fingers carding through my hair, making my eyes heavy.

"You should let me remove those with tweezers," he whispered, his tender massage of my sweaty scalp soothing beyond words.

"Nah, I'm fine. I once played out the end of a period

with a broken ankle. This little bit of glass? Pfft. It's nothing." He paid me no mind and, within a few minutes was watching as I hoisted my ass up off the floor. My briefs were wet from the seltzer, so I peeled them off before I stood and tossed them over the broken bulb. "We can vacuum that up in a bit," I told whoever might be listening, my pulse finally down to normal levels. Balancing on one leg was becoming easier and easier every day. Cooper moved over for me. I sat down, and he shifted around to face me, his legs crossed, a first aid kit on his lap.

"Are you okay?" he timidly asked while opening his little white box with the red cross on the lid. "Emotionally. I know you're a tough man who played a whole game with a spear lodged in your skull, but—" I snorted in amusement. He gave me a perturbed look over the top of lemon frames. "But even so. Stop picking at it. That's how infections start. I know where you had those fingers last."

"You should." The dark look intensified. "You're cute when you worry."

"Stop it. Tell me if you're okay emotionally or not. Shall I call down to your floor for Phillippe?"

"No, gods, no. He'll be dragging me off to another therapist for dream analysis or scrubbing or whatever. I can't talk to any more people right now. I'm at my 'relate the trauma' limit. Just dig them out and dump some peroxide on them." I jerked my scruffy chin at my forearm. He did not look amused, but he began tweezing teensy bits of glass from my arm.

Penelope, thank goodness, slept in the living room on a bed fit for Princess Anne. Cooper wasn't fond of dog hairs in his ears. We'd found one after a few days of him saying a termite was in his head. After that, he didn't want to sleep with her head on his pillow anymore, or her hairs in his bedroom. Which was totally understandable. She was on the other side of the door, whimpering softly to be let in.

"Go back to bed," I called, and with a theatrical sigh, the dog moved off. "You do good work."

He was methodical, that was for sure. Me and my brother would have just run the backside of a hunting knife on the slivers, like a bee stinger, and called it good. Cooper was bent over his crossed legs, his brow furrowed, diligently removing every tiny bit of glass.

"I don't want to leave any behind." He looked up, his eyes filled with worry. "When was the last bad nightmare?"

"Oh gosh, it's been a good month or so. That's improvement. They used to be every night. Maybe it was the movie we watched." I shrugged. "No clue what triggers them. You don't have to use iodine on each scratch." I didn't want to let him know how bad that burned because I was a tough man with a spear in my head and all that. "I'll wash when… okay, you go ahead and use that iodine then." I sighed to cover up a hiss. Fuck: that shit stung.

"I'm glad I was here with you."

"I wish you weren't." His face fell. "Oh no, not like that, baby. I just would hate to lash out and hurt you. If I caught you in the nose…" The thought of that made me ill.

"I think having me here was beneficial. To that end, you should be in my bed until the dreams stop completely." He plucked a shard free and dropped it into the lid of the first aid kit.

"That might take years, Cooper. It might never happen. I might be this big, dumb ginger bear of a man flailing around in your bed until I crash another plane or wreck a car or get hit in the head by a meteor, then die."

He shook his head, and his gaze flew to mine. "That won't happen. I've done the calculations, and given the fact that you've survived a plane crash, I feel safe in my predictions that the vagaries of the universe will align to keep you on this plane for at least several more eons."

"Two things." He glanced down to dump more iodine on another cut. Ouch and motherfucker. "One, is that I'm dumbfounded you are talking about vagaries of life and fate and all that kind of metaphysical shit. And two, is me asking if you want me in your bed for several eons."

"Oh. Well, I…" He swallowed, his tweezers pausing, thank Christ. "It's more statistical, than mystical. The odds that something horribly big will befall you are lower since you've already plummeted to the Earth in a tiny plane and lived. While it is true, some people do get struck by lightning numerous times, I rather like to think that's due to being on a hill or such in the thunderstorm. Bad timing and all that."

"And for me in your bed for eons?" I prodded just a bit. It was fun to see him blush.

"I'd like that." He said no more, just went back to tweezing and dousing. Ouch and fucking ouch.

"I'd like that too." He glanced up, smiled, and reached for the iodine. "I'm not a real fan of that stuff though, if I can—ouch!"

"Big tough hockey player," I heard him mumble under his breath.

I lunged for him, tipping the first aid kit and the iodine all over the bed. He giggled, snorted, and then went lax in my arms, as I loved his worries and giggles away.

FOUR DAYS BEFORE CHRISTMAS, TONY, COOPER, AND I went on a shopping/PR excursion. Phillippe and his wife had gone home, with hugs, kisses, and lots of winks for me and Cooper, to spend the holidays in Nunavut, as they did every year. Piita had gone back home to finish out his season, scouts drooling over the skilled forward.

The shopping part of the day went well. I wore my prosthetic all day—the new walking blade from Cooper—and with the help of my funky metal cane, I strolled through several stores picking up things for everyone at the tower, from the doorman to Cooper himself.

After a filling lunch at Salty Sal's Seafood on the harbor, we made our way to the rink to meet up with the Rebels newly-formed sled team, the Stripes. Named after the striper, which is a fish in Boston Harbor, or so they told me. Several of the Rebels had signed on to volunteer their time, but with the season in high gear, that time would be limited. On the other hand, I had nothing but time. Something about the experience was making me edgy. Even as I walked into the rink with only a slight limp, my nerves were on edge.

"You look like you're ready to run off," Cooper noted as we made our way to the ice. The rink was a small one, but nicely fitted for hockey and figure skating. I paused by a ramp leading down to the ice, my sight flicking over Tony's head to the men down below.

"I've never been around so many guys who are missing limbs," I confessed, whispering so only Cooper would hear me -- embarrassed to confide that to anyone -- but I knew Cooper would understand. He also had issues with social interactions at times. "I know that sounds awful, but this makes me feel like... like if I get into this, then I'm admitting that I'm an amputee."

"Well, you are." Yep. There was that frankness that I so admired. "There's no shame in that. It's just what you are. I'm autistic. Tony is overprotective."

"I heard that," Tony called from a few feet away. The man had ears like an owl.

"I guess, I've been living this fantasy that if I worked hard enough, no one would consider me disabled. But I will be."

"Only if you think of yourself that way."

I stared down at the man with the polka dot frames, bright red beanie, and cherry red nose. I loved how red his nose got when he was cold. That was only one of many things that I adored about him, but now was not the time.

"You're incredibly smart," I said, stooping down to brush a kiss over his ruddy cheeks.

"I know. So, shall we go meet the team?" He took off without me. I chuckled, shook my head, and followed along at my gimpy clip. Marquis, Lomac, Austin, and Joachim all hooted and clapped when I finally made it to the ice. "Yeah, yeah, I know, slow as molasses in January.

You'd think I'd be faster, since I got me an extra leg or two."

Everyone laughed, me the loudest, as I held up my skating leg over my head and let loose a cry like a Tusken warrior. The *Star Wars* fans on the ice—and there were several—all replied in kind, and I knew I'd found my people.

Lomac was everywhere I looked. And sometimes seeing him just made me feel... small? No, maybe not small. Old. A has-been. Like, I know he was trying to prove himself, but did he have to shine so much on *my* team? Or was that just me feeling washed-up? Shit. That was something I was going to have to work on. Feeling inadequate was a new thing for me. Maybe now it was time to start whittling that away. I wasn't inadequate at all. I was just a new version of Dunny. Time to start remembering that.

———

IT WAS DARK BEFORE WE LEFT THE RINK. I'D SPENT AN hour on the ice playing hockey. I sucked. Really badly. And my stump ached like a bitch. But I was playing hockey. And so were a bunch of other guys missing limbs. Some had been firemen, cops, and military. Some had lost their limbs to accidents, disease, or birth defects. Every man on the ice had been a warrior. They'd not stopped living after becoming amputees. I found great courage and determination on the team that the Rebels were assembling. And they'd found themselves a new coach.

"You look festive," Cooper said from the back of his limo as we crawled through evening rush hour.

"I feel festive. Thank you for talking me into going."

He snuggled into my side. Tony muttered under his breath as he steered us through the infamous Boston gridlock. I draped an arm around his shoulder, buried my face into his knitted cap, and just breathed him in.

"Since I took the offer to coach the sled team, I guess I'll be staying in Boston instead of heading back to Canada," I tossed out just to test the waters.

"I'd like that," he said, then his head shot up from my shoulder. "But we are going to your cabin to see the Northern Lights, right? I have a new folder made for my notes while we're there."

"Oh yeah, we're totally going. As soon as I get my final fittings done. I got me a nice place by the barn that I'll be moving back into. There's no reason for me to be in your tower once I'm up and running." And I would be running. Hell, I was now. Not at the Flash speed, but I was running and walking, and playing motherfucking hockey. Oh, and I was crazy in love with the most amazing ladybug loving scientist. "I mean, unless you want Penelope and me to stay in the tower with you."

He let his eyes drift shut as we moved along. I held him close and let him work through what I'd just put on the table.

SEVENTEEN

Cooper

THE NEXT MORNING, I WANTED TO SIT IN SILENCE AND make a pros and cons list, and work my way through what Moral had said— instead, Tony and his family were up in my space to swim. I know I'd invited them, but part of me —the part that didn't want chaos and noise—was dreading this moment and had been pleased each time they'd canceled for one reason or another. Moral suggested that Tony didn't want to blur the lines between bodyguard and family man, but I knew it was just because the kids and I would probably freak each other out.

But the worst was imagining a time *after-Moral*, when he inevitably moved on.

It's happened before.

When I was six, I re-homed the school turtle after this kid, Mikey something, tried to feed it pizza. Some later accused me of stealing it, but I had merely re-homed Leonardo because he looked lonely. I set up this awesome terrarium in my grandmother's old basement to give Leonardo somewhere to live, and Gramma didn't care what I was doing down there. Mom and Dad were away, and I loved my new friend. Actually, he was my *only* friend at that time, not that I had a proper concept of friendship back then. Even now, I wonder if I still don't understand friendship in its real sense. Even though I know that Brianna and Tony and Uncle Jeremiah, plus Moral now, are all important people, I know I'm a hard worker and they have to make most of the allowances for me. Still, they stayed with me. Not that Uncle Jeremiah had a choice, given that he'd been my legal guardian. Anyway, Leonardo-the-turtle lived very happily with me...

Until I brought him back into school for show and tell.

I never understood why everyone was so freaked out, and I never got labeled a thief, or told that I'd done wrong.

No one seemed interested when I told them about Mikey and the pizza feeding incident.

They didn't give Leonardo back to me, and I was labeled a freak and a weirdo at school.

I didn't care about the labels or the people who shoved at me.

I just missed Leonardo.

But I knew my family felt awful for me, that they were sad, and that made me sad and confused, and then the kids who taunted me were upsetting my family.

Leonardo had lived briefly with me, somewhere safe, where he was loved. Moral was offering me the same thing —time for us to be happy together. Only...

What if *they* took him back, or rather, what if just when everything felt right, he left? Or was taken from me?

"Hi."

I glanced down, and then further down, Tony's

youngest—a girl, five years old—Abigail, Abby for short, was standing in front of me, staring up and holding out what looked like a spinning top that lit up from inside. She was in a ballerina skirt, a miniature Rebels jersey that Moral had gifted her, her long blond hair up in bunches like rabbit ears, and she wrinkled her nose at me.

"It won't do it." She held out her tiny palm and in the middle sat a very dead looking toy. "Fix it."

I glanced over at Tony, who was at the opposite side of the pool, staring at me. Why wasn't he over here saving me from small children?

"I'm not sure—"

"Daddy said fix it."

"He can fix everything." Moral was suddenly next to me putting an arm over my shoulders.

"Not everything," I defended and wondered why Tony had sent his daughter to me of all people. "I couldn't fix the laser yesterday that was—"

"Fix it?" little Abby interrupted. She wiggled the spinner again, and something compelled me to take it. Maybe it was Moral's defense saying I could fix anything, or the way the little girl was staring at me as if I might be her hero or something.

"I'll have a look," I said, nearly yelping when she took my hand.

"I wanna watch."

To my credit, I didn't tug my hand away, and thankfully, as I went to sit at the table by the pool, hand in hand with my newest friend, Moral came with us. I poked a finger in the hole left by the loose plastic part and felt around for something to attach it to. There wasn't anything

I could feel, and I poked some more, finally finding a connector and a clip and once I located the other half of it, the fix was easy, but as I clicked it together, it worried me that a toy meant for kids had an issue if things could come loose so easily.

I glanced up at Abby and she was flapping her hands, staring at the spinner with an intense look of concentration. She took the spinner and flicked a switch, staring at the lights inside with utter focus. I didn't always recognize the signs in other people, but when I glanced back up at Tony, he gave me a nod.

Abby was autistic.

The same as me.

I wondered if she had friends. Or wanted friends. Would she get to my age and be scarred, and scared into thinking that people would always want to leave them? Tony and his wife seemed like good parents, and I knew they'd always be there for her. But my parents never *planned* on leaving me. They never planned on a volcano erupting when they were trapped too close, and they didn't mean to die. What if someone shot at me, and Tony did what he was paid for, took a bullet for me. What if he died, then little Abby would have no one in her corner?

"I'll always be here to fix your things," I blurted, and she glanced up at me and back at the spinning toy. Then, she grabbed it and clambered down off the seat.

"Thank you," she said prettily and skipped over to her dad. My big, strong ninja bodyguard scooped up his little princess and swung her around. I made a mental note to mention the safety issue with the toy and realized that Moral was staring at me.

"What?" I asked.

"I love you," Moral murmured, lacing his fingers with mine. His touch settled me, centered me, made me feel as if I could do this crazy thing that was life.

"She has autism."

"So Tony said."

"He never told me. But I never asked, did I?"

"Don't be too hard on yourself."

"I stole a turtle."

"What? When?" He looked at the ground as if he expected a turtle to go sauntering by and was clearly unfazed by the change in direction.

"A long time ago."

"You stole a turtle? Tell me everything?"

A loud splash as Tony's boy, Bradley, jumped into the pool, distracted me, and made me smile when I realized I wasn't stressing about it, but loved the whooping sound as he broke the surface. The pool just saw me with my unending lengths and Moral with his inflatables—it deserved more fun.

I told Moral about Leonardo and pizza and the kidnapping. And how Leonardo had been my only friend, and how it hurt when they took him away, and he grew slowly quieter. Was I making sense with this story and explaining how I felt about people leaving me?

"So that's why I worry about living with you all the time," I summarized, and he nodded.

"Because someone might take me away?"

"No, because you don't have to have anyone taking you away. You could just leave."

"I won't leave."

I snorted a laugh. "You can't promise that!"

"Okay, maybe not... hmmm... how about I promise you that wherever we live—and I can guarantee you, we will make that happen, so get used to it—I will never leave for good if we don't agree on it first."

"So, before leaving me, you mean we could make a pros and cons list first?" That sounded like the very best idea I could think of. He smiled at me, and the smile crinkled his eyes.

"That sounds like the best idea," he agreed and leaned forward to kiss me.

"And you wouldn't mind moving in here with Penelope? I have the space, but it's not a proper home."

He smiled into another kiss. "I think a home could be wherever we are together."

Another splash from Bradley, this time with Tony, and the water flooded over Moral and me. I was grinning, and I didn't care. "Then... move in?"

"I'm already packed."

OUR FIRST NIGHT OFFICIALLY TOGETHER WAS ALSO THE evening that the Rebels came to test out the new ice. They were between two home games. They'd lost the first against a hot Florida team, so Moral told me, and the second was tomorrow against Dallas. They were going to win against Dallas, again, so Moral told me, and then he grumbled about how the team was shit without him. He called his therapist when he caught himself doing that, and even though he seemed lighter after the call, he was still grumpy and stressed.

Not because of moving in, but because of the Rebels visiting.

I hoped.

Marquis was the first to arrive, with a blond man behind him who said his name was Kaleb. I didn't know Kaleb, although I knew Marquis was with him and they were happy. Austin Rowe appeared, and he was on his own, but grinned broadly and thrust some beers at me. I liked Marquis and Austin.

"I'd like to talk about your sand batteries." Kaleb cornered me by the snacks laid out next to the rink.

"You would?" I probably sounded surprised, but to be honest, not many people I'd met through Moral wanted to talk efficient energy storage solutions. I lost myself in a very pleasant few minutes of chatting with him, and he listened as I rambled on about upscaling solar energy, and consequently, found out he was a prince. Which was cool.

"You should visit Norstoe," he said, just as Moral came up next to me and hugged me close.

"I'd love to."

"Love to what?" Moral asked and frowned. "Don't fall for his royal flirting."

"I wasn't flirting, ass," Prince Kaleb shook his head, "we were discussing energy storage in sand batteries."

"Which is totally flirting where my man is concerned." Moral pressed a kiss to my head.

"I was just inviting you to Norstoe." Kaleb smiled at Marquis as he joined us, then grinned widely. "You could sleep in the crypt again."

Marquis shuddered at that. "Freaking ghosts," he muttered.

"You have ghosts? You actually have recorded evidence of paranormal activity?" Now I was intrigued. Of all the black and white opinions I held, the existence of ghosts was well outside of them, but also intriguing.

"And we're done," Moral said, guiding me away from Kaleb, who for some reason was waggling his hands and making wooooowoooo sounds at Moral. I don't know what it was about Kaleb doing that, but I couldn't help laughing. "Laugh it up, fuzzball," he quipped.

"Is that a new pet name for me?" I asked.

"Don't tell me you've never seen *Star Wars* either."

"Nope. We can watch that when we're up to date with the James Bond movies."

By this time, we'd made it to the seats, and Moral sat down and began to remove what he called his street-blade, and I waited as he carefully replaced it with the ice-blade. That was when the worries hit me.

"You won't let them hit you, right?" Seemingly on cue, the door to the basement opened and a group of six walked in, all talking and laughing and brimming with testosterone. I immediately shrank in my seat, but next to me Moral sat upright and let out a whoop worthy of Bradley whenever he jumped in the pool.

I was introduced to a ton of people, a cousin of Austin's who played for Florida and was still in town, Xander, Joachim, and Kyle, and others. They were all so boisterous around Moral, which made me nervous. Each of them shook my hand with quiet respect, and I liked them for that, but then they were immediately back on, helping

Moral out to the ice, and joking with him. The last person to turn up was someone whom I recognized from my research and from Moral's ramblings—Lomac—Logan Mackie. He seemed hesitant to walk in, but after a pause where he inhaled deeply and fiddled with his jacket, he smiled at everyone and sauntered over as if he didn't have a care in the world. I might not be the best at reading people, but Moral was noticeably quiet when he chatted to Lomac, which disappeared when they were all on the ice.

The entire group began to skate, not speeding, not with drama, but in slow lazy loops, still chatting, ribbing Moral as he wobbled a couple of times, but all of them were there and ready to catch him if he fell. I hope he didn't notice that too much because he'd hate to be pitied or mothered, but he never stopped smiling. They'd all brought sticks with them, and they'd given Moral one, and for the first time he was skating with a stick, unable to use his arms for balance.

It was terrifying to watch.

I couldn't wait until tonight, seeing his things hanging next to mine, knowing that we would be sharing a bed, and this was forever.

So, I drank my soda, ate some popcorn, and watched my man do his thing.

EIGHTEEN

Moral

THE NEXT MONTH FLEW BY WITH A SPEED THAT LEFT ME A little dizzy.

Or maybe that spinning top feeling was due to being so in love with Cooper.

Whatever the cause, I was now jogging on the treadmill with my running blade.

I was walking across the room without a cane.

I'd sent the wheelchair to a charity that would give it to someone in need.

And I was skating.

Skating.

Yeah, it wasn't with the Rebels. Obviously. But I was with the Rebels sled team, and my speed was improving. As was my balance. The team played once a month, league weekend they called it, but had practices every Saturday morning at eight sharp. I'd been attending for a few weeks now, and the guys on the Rebels would show up when they could. On this bright and chilly January morning, it was me, the guys on the sled team who were freaking awesome fellas, and one Logan Mackie.

Yeah.

I was trying my level best to be nice to the guy. Guess I was failing because, after a sweaty skate and practice, I was having a long chat with Jim Choy, the director of business operations for the sled team about next season, when I spotted Lomac chilling by the Zamboni doors, scrolling on his phone as his gaze rested on me. Well shit.

"… love to have you in the organization," Jim was saying when I snapped back to the talk that I'd been hoping to have. "You bring a real fire to the club, and you've played professionally, which we hope will give us an edge. We're a competitive bunch."

"I've seen that. I would love to take part in any way that I can," I replied with a smile. We shook hands, Jim's grin eating up his whole face, and then he hurried off to talk to someone in the organization about a future contract for me as a coach. Feeling about the best that I had felt since that day I did my Icarus imitation, I skated out of the sled hockey bench area and over to Lomac.

"You waiting for a date?" I asked him.

"Nah, waiting for you," he replied and slid his phone into the back pocket of his jeans. "Can we talk?"

I nodded and motioned to the home bench. We glided over, took a seat, and sat there looking uncomfortable until I spoke up.

"Look, I know what this is about." He glanced at me with pretty blue eyes. The guy was a real looker. If I weren't crazy ga-ga over Cooper, I'd probably hit on him.

Well, maybe not. He did usurp me. Damn it. No. No, he did not. "I'm sorry for being an ass the past few months."

"No, hey, it's cool. I get it. And I was just going to tell you that if me being here is making you uncomfortable that I was going to stop volunteering. I'm used to moving on."

"Yeah, no, do not do that," I quickly said. I saw the shock in his eyes. "Seriously, don't leave. This is a great program, and they need volunteers. I'd feel like shit if you left because of me being a jerk."

"You've not been—"

I cut him right off. "Yeah, I have been. I know it. I see it. My boyfriend sees it. The world sees it." I inhaled and let the breath out through my mouth, my cheeks ballooning. "Okay so it's like this, right? Say you've been dating this girl for years..."

"Or guy," he slipped in, and I nodded.

"Right or guy. Or ferret. Whatever tickles your goolies. Point being, so you've been dating this person for years, and no one else." I ran my hands over my jogging pants, my fingers sliding down over my knees, rubbing at the stump and my good knee. I'd been on the skating blade for over two hours, and there was soreness. "So you and this person are tight. You feel that this is the one, the true love of your life, and you start making plans with them to be lifelong companions. Then, one day, you come home, and they tell you they still care about you, and always will, but they don't want to be a part of your life anymore. While you're still reeling from that news, they inform you that they found someone else to fill the space. Someone who can easily take your place, blonder, and with all his limbs, and that they're going to be with him."

"Shit, man." Lomac sighed, his shoulders drooping, self-consciously skimming a hand through his hair.

"Hey, no see here. Listen, all of that isn't on you. And it's not on the team. And it's not on me. It's just hockey, right?" He gave me a halfhearted nod. "No, it is, and you know it. The team replaced me. They had to. I'm done playing professional hockey. I wouldn't have wanted them to keep me on. Kind of like when you know your girl or guy isn't happy, so you give them permission to move on. Only, like, I gave the team the okay to let me go, but I kept pissing on the new guy's tires."

His head came up. "You pissed on my tires?!"

"Nah, man, metaphorically speaking. I've been a jerk to you. That's not the way I want to be anymore. It's not professional. You did nothing wrong, true? You didn't steal my position. You earned that spot fair and square. You're a good player, damn good on the team, so good I reckon they might offer you longer term."

"You think?" He seemed surprised, but then he was a rental, someone who moved onto teams that had temporary spaces. It was a hard job to do.

"Sure. And yeah, I'll do better. Don't bail on account of my stupid mooseheadedness."

"Is that even a word?"

"Sure is. You ain't from Canada, so you don't know, but mooseheadedness is for sure a word. Look it up," I teased and got a smile from him. "Nah, it ain't a real word, I totally made it up, but it fits. I can be stubborn as a moose at times. Thickskulled too. My family will attest to that for sure." I glanced from my skates to Lomac. "So we good?"

"Yeah, man, we are super good." He offered me his hand. I slapped my palm over his and shook hard. He did the same. "I know you don't like to hear this, but I think you're incredibly brave." I rolled my eyes, dropping his hand to massage my aching stump. "You are. Coming back like this couldn't have been easy. Shit, everyone on this sled team is a damn hero. Battling back when it would be so much easier to just give up? That's real courage."

"Nah, not for me, it ain't. For them," I waved at the area that the sled team players rested in when they were changing lines, "for them, yeah. They're all heroes. Cops, firemen, military, those born with issues."

"Right, and several who lost limbs to accidents. Just. Like. You." He bumped the side of my good leg with his fist.

"Maybe."

"Man, you *are* mooseheaded."

That made me snort. "Told you." I gave him a fist to bump. Which he did. "So you going to pick up all the cones out there or you going to make the guy with the fake leg do it?"

"Oh my God, that was so damn low!"

"Yeah, I know. It would have worked, too, if I wasn't such a stand-up kind of guy." I waited for a beat. "Get it? Stand-up guy? I'm missing a leg?"

"Dude," he gasped. Right. I'd have to tell that one to Cooper. He'd get it.

"Let's do this," I said as he gaped at me.

He rose. I did as well.
We cleaned up together.

NINETEEN

Cooper

I WAS SUPER NERVOUS. NOT JUST THE RUN OF THE MILL nervous like before a dentist appointment or something, but full on worried that I was about to mess Moral's birthday up.

"Where are we going?" Moral asked for the fifth time as I guided his blindfolded self, past an office area and into the development studio for EdGoTech engineering. Cutting edge experts in carbon fiber race car design, they were the first people to come up with a workable solution for what I wanted for Moral, and today was the big unveiling.

I just hope he didn't kill me.

After all, he said he didn't want anyone touching his cars. Not even I was allowed to touch them, and I got away with most things where Moral was concerned. I stopped at the best vantage point and cleared my throat.

"You can take the blindfold off," I said.

He lifted the material, but he had his eyes screwed shut. "And can I open my eyes?"

Oh yeah, I'd made him do both—just in case. "Sure, sorry, of course." Now I was fumbling my words, so far outside of my comfort zone that I was about to have a meltdown. I caught Tony's concerned gaze and sent him a smile of reassurance because I was sure I could handle whatever Moral's reaction was once the dust settled.

At least I thought I was sure.

Love made my head all prickly sometimes when I thought I'd messed things up—maybe I was messing this up now.

"Okay, I'm opening them," Moral said, and did so, blinking in the light that bounced off the white painted floor and walls. After a moment he stopped the rapid blinking and then his mouth fell open.

What did he see? Did he see his beautiful Ferrari destroyed by the addition and removal of all kinds of things, *or* his beautiful Ferrari better than it was before because now he'd be able to drive it?

"What did you do?" Moral asked in an even tone. He didn't sound pissed, but he didn't exactly sound pleased. Staring at his face, I tried to find a reaction that made sense.

"I worked with the tech firm to adapt the car so you can use it without the..." I stopped because I got the uncomfortable feeling that he didn't actually want to know what we'd done to his baby. I think it was one of those rhetorical questions that sometimes eluded me. *Not everyone needs an essay on process.*

"I can get in?"

"Huh?"

"I can get into the car?" He glanced at me, and I

nodded. Without hesitation, he approached the driver's side and took a key from the technical expert I'd been dealing with, a short skinny kid called Edgar who was literally an automotive genius. He unlocked the door and pulled it open, leaning in and inhaling deeply. The seats were leather, and the whole car had been detailed from top to bottom, and the scent inside was intoxicating. I could see why Moral loved the car so much, from its shiny scarlet exterior to the cocoon inside. He was examining the floor now, and abruptly stepped back, stumbling a little and, then, righting himself.

"You need to come here," he muttered and pointed at himself.

I hurried around as fast as I could, ready with all kinds of answers and justifications, and didn't get any of them out when he tugged me close and kissed me.

Right in front of Tony, who was used to it, and Eddie Goff—efficiency personified—was probably shocked at us kissing in his pristine workspace.

I eased away and searched Moral's eyes for a reaction. "You're not angry with me?" I asked quickly. "I know you said that your car shouldn't be touched, but I—"

He kissed me again to shut me up. He'd learned that lesson and used it well.

This time when we parted, me out of breath, and him smiling, I got the feeling that maybe I'd done something right.

"This is the best gift you could have gotten me," Moral said, and his eyes were bright with emotion.

"For real?"

"For real."

"You'll need some training on how to use the controls, but I can call someone to get them over if you want me to. They're dual so someone without a prosthetic can drive also."

He hugged me close. "Not yet, but soon, yeah? For now, I just want to take her home, look at her and love on her a bit. Can Tony drive her home?"

Tony was front and center in an instant, looking like a kid in a candy store. "I can if you need me to. I'll call backup for you, and we'll get her home."

I loved how Moral and Tony stared at the car with the same kind of reverence I had for my experiments.

Part one went okay, part two was something bigger for me, and something I hoped would help Moral understand me even more.

"What are we watching?" Moral yawned as he sat next to me on the sofa, removing his prosthetic and unrolling the support before slumping back. It had been a busy day what with the car, and then polishing the car, and then staring at the car with any Rebel that decided to visit, not to mention Moral's family, and most of the staff in the building. Finally, it was the two of us, his favorite Poutine polished off, and candles on a tiny cake long since blown out.

"You should probably meet my parents," I murmured, and settled back next to him.

"You found the documentary?"

"I've always had it. I've just never watched it since… y'know… I've never watched it." I have photos of my parents. Luckily, Uncle Jeremiah was never short of a story about my dad or my mom, only this was different—this was actual moving and talking images.

"You don't have to if you don't want to," Moral reminded me, and I knew that, but for now, I wanted to give him a gift of knowing who I was and where I came from, and it felt right.

The documentary started, and after the introduction with stills of my parents, of Uncle Jeremiah with me standing next to him, plus dramatic images of a looming volcano behind, it expanded to give background of my parents.

And Uncle Jeremiah.

And me.

After the first few seconds of it, Moral tugged me onto his lap, and I curled up against his chest and waited for the flood of emotions to take me under. Instead, because he was holding me, it was okay to watch the life story of my parents and the disaster that claimed thirty-seven, my parents included.

"… for that single day, the younger Harvey, Cooper, stayed at base, and for that reason he was saved. Cooper Harvey went on to discover the properties to form Coopersil, the base for blankets now used by volcanologists and fire fighters alike to protect from fire. The last photo taken of his parents is haunting as they smile and wave up at their son, never knowing that—"

The TV went black, and I realized Moral had turned it off.

"Why did you stop it?" I asked.

"Because it was going to focus on the sad parts of you being you, and I don't want *you* to have to see them. And

I'm not sorry, if I've gone into protection mode, because I love you and one day we'll watch it all, but right now, I just want to hold you and tell you that you're all safe and okay. Is that okay?" His voice was thick with emotion, and I never meant to upset him on his birthday.

"I'm sorry, I just, I wanted you to see where I came from."

"I get that." He sighed heavily and cleared his throat. "But, sweetheart, I don't have to know how they died to see them in you."

"Really?"

"You look like your mom." He spoke softly into my hair.

"Thank you. She was beautiful."

"But you have your dad's smile."

That was a comforting thought—my dad smiled in all the photos I had. A familiar grief curled in my chest, but I'd shared this with Moral, and now he knew all the parts of me.

"I love you, Moral," I whispered, and he tightened his hold on me.

"I love you too. And maybe in a few weeks I can drive us around in my flashy car?"

"I'd like that."

"But first… bed for a birthday snuggle?"

"And more?" I teased and hoped at the same time.

"Way more."

I never moved so fast.

Epilogue

MORAL

"OH! COME OVER HERE AND LOOK AT IT NOW."

I rolled to my side, super warm and comfy, and smiled at Cooper with his head poking outside of the tent. Again.

"I saw it just ten minutes ago. And ten minutes before that. And ten minutes before that. Has it changed much?" I propped my head up with my hand, enjoying the view of Coop's pert backside in those snowflake sleeping pants of his. He was resting on his heels, his head fully outside of the tent. His backside looked pretty edible, with that bright white and blue cotton stretched over it. I reached out and gave him a goose. He yelped, squealed, and flung about, tumbling back into my arms, but leaving the window flap open on our spacious tent.

"That scared me." He giggled as I rolled him to his back, my lips hungry for a taste of his.

"Nothing to be scared of. You're with a mountain man. I'll protect you from anything roaming around out there."

I stole a kiss.

Someone rapped on the back of the tent. "Boss, you okay in there?"

"It's all fine, Tony. Moral grabbed my butt cheek. Go back to your tent. Tell the kids to be ready to investigate the hiking trails tomorrow. I brought some wonderful binoculars and we should be able to spot several species of winter birds to add to our notebooks."

"Will do, boss." Tony moved away, his footfalls in the crunchy snow fading off as he made his way back to his tent. Actually, tent is kind of a misnomer. These massive things we were camping in reminded me more of a circus big top than my old Scouts Canada single sleeper. Cooper said it was called "glamping" whatever the shit that was. All I knew was that when a tent had a stove, a queen bed, and a martini bar, it wasn't what this Canuck called camping.

"I'm getting cold," Cooper whispered and sat up to tie down the window flap over our bed. I stole a quick peek at the sky, the Aurora Borealis painting the ebony blackness with glowing shades of emerald that melted into sapphire. The sight never failed to impress. Kind of like my man's warm laugh or the way he moved when sitting astride me, his sleek body pleasing me as no lover ever had before. "There. Do you think Phillippe and Yuka will want to come along?"

"I don't know. She's not feeling so good in the mornings of late. Maybe they can skip this walk?" I held up the thick blankets that Brianna had ensured would be on all the beds, hoping he would shimmy under and put his cold little bottom against my stiff dick. "Uncle Jeremiah can take their place. He missed the walk today."

"I told him to not sip so much brandy last night. You look tired." He sat down beside me, the light from the portable propane heater throwing a warm orange glow on the inside of our tent. "You should give yourself some rest during the day."

"I'm good. Just achy. Stump hurts. Too long with the prosthetic. I'll be fine." I stretched out with a yawn. He pulled back the cover over my left leg, frowned, and plucked the bottle of lotion from the tiny nightstand. A nightstand. In a tent. I'd never seen such luxury. You'd think Marquis and his prince were camping up here behind my cabin given all the fancy accoutrements and entourage. "Hey, no, I can do that, baby."

Penelope lifted her head from the plush doggie bed by the stove, snuffled at us, and then resumed snoring. I glanced back from the dog to Cooper.

"I know." He squirted some lotion into his hands, rubbed them together, and then gently placed his palms on my left knee. A sigh escaped me. "Just relax and let me do this for you."

"Okay, baby, okay." I let my shoulders slump back to the mattress and closed my eyes. This was a new thing for us. Him massaging my stump nightly. Sometimes, I freaking loved it and sometimes I wanted to cringe. I knew that was all the stuff in my head, the self-doubt about myself, my scars, and my missing limb trying to insinuate itself back into my psyche. His touch was feather light at first, then he began working the flesh, his hands warming as he kneaded away the pain. I groaned in pleasure. "Damn, that feels so good tonight."

"You overdid it. We didn't have to try out the skiing prosthetic today. That could have waited."

"Nah, it was good. Great even! Give me a couple more runs on it, and I'll out-ski all of you." He began talking about mechanics and skiing and speed and… I didn't know what else. My mind kind of drifted as he chattered. My thoughts floated around the inside of the tent, picking up the hiss of the stove, the slight rustle of cold air blowing over the air vents, and the slight creak of the bed as he moved this way and that. Bouncing along in that gossamer place between wakefulness and sleep, I did as he asked, lifting my leg to allow him to massage the back of my knee, then up my thigh. He talked steadily, his voice soft and mellow, the sound like waves on the shore.

"I love your body," he whispered against my leg, his breath a warm puff that made my hairs stand on end. I purred like a fat cat in a soft chair when he began kissing down the inside of my thigh, his fingers roaming up and down my leg. "It's so strong. Thick. Beefy."

With that, he pressed his cheek to my leg, then ever-so-gently kissed my stump. My eyes followed him, my shoulders tensing, as I waited for the revulsion to overtake his face. It never did, though. He peppered my knee with tiny little pecks and worked his way back up, his lips grazing the underside of my cock before he sucked me into his mouth. My hips came up sharply, the glory of that hot, wet heat searing me inside and out. Knowing he didn't like to have my hands on his head when he was giving me a blowjob, I fisted the covers instead, letting my eyes rest on him as he bobbed up and down, his dark eyes on me as he brought me to the edge and then over in no time flat. My body shuddered violently, cum flooding his mouth as he hummed in pleasure and swallowed a few times.

"Oh hell... baby," I panted, reaching down for him, my hands gliding under his slim arms to pull him over top of me. His mouth slanted over mine. I moved to the side, tossed my left leg over his hip, and wiggled my hand down into his snowflake pants. "Your turn."

"I love when it's... ah, oh your hands are so rough."

"Sorry, baby," I whispered as I stroked his length. His lips were pink and slick, my taste lingering on his tongue, as I kissed him long and hard. He pumped into my hand, his cock weeping over my palm when I gave his rosy head a twist.

"I want to come now. Right now. Moral... please," he said against my lips.

"Then come for me, baby," I gruffly replied, tugging him hard and quick. He went stiff, his white teeth latching onto my shoulder, his cock kicking. Thick spunk coated my hand, easing his thrusts even more. He trembled and gasped. I captured his whimpers with a kiss, keeping the bodyguard sleeping ten feet away from hearing it and making another trip through the snow to see if his charge was safe. "Mm, that's so pretty," I said, watching as he drifted back from the heavens.

He smiled dreamily. His brown eyes were sleepy with pleasure. "I really like it when you do that. Your hands are so big and calloused. So different from mine."

"I love it when you come apart in my arms." I placed a tiny peck on the tip of his nose. He yawned, rolled to his back, and removed his glasses. Pink frames with little yellow dots this time. He snuggled into the bedding, his knees drawn up, his pert bottom sticking out. I moved to the edge of the bed, sat up, and used my toes to pull my discarded T-shirt over to me.

"My butt is getting cold," he informed me. I reached back to pat his backside, then wiped the jizz from my fingers.

"Not sure how it could be cold. It's like Palm Beach in here."

That was no lie.

"Can we see it one more time?"

I sighed and reached up to open the window flap over the bed before burrowing back under the covers. He flipped to his back and tipped his head up. I lay beside him, staring at his beauty, instead of the natural phenomena overhead.

"Gosh, how beautiful is that? Did you know the lights are caused by electrons entering the Earth's atmosphere where they collide with nitrogen and oxygen molecules, sending them into a frenzied state? When the excited electrons calm down, they release light. I love science."

"I know you do," I softly said, watching the mysterious lights in the sky as they danced. I looked to the side. He looked at me, his smile a gentle, loving one that did all kinds of things to me. "You know what I love more than science?"

"Root beer floats?" I shook my head. "Gummy bears?" Another shake. "Poutine?"

"Okay, I *do* love poutine, but do you know what I love more than poutine?"

"Me?"

"Yep. You."

He moved to his side, snuggled into my chest, and sighed as if he had found heaven. "I love you more than poutine, too."

Peeking up at me, his lips curled at the edges. I couldn't help stealing a kiss. Or two. Or ten. Or twenty.

"You think our love makes us so excited that we make light just like the Aurora does?" I teased and got a snuffle-snort from the man curled into my arms. "Let's get excited again and see. I bet we light up this whole mountainside."

"That's preposterous," he stated, but his hands began to move over my body. "But we should see if we do. Purely for scientific purposes." He winked.

I moved to my back, and he crawled over me, his mouth sliding over mine.

By the time we fell asleep, spent and utterly exhausted, I was pretty sure they could see our love light all the way to Ottawa.

THE END

What's next for the Rebels?

Rental (Boston Rebels 6)

Love doesn't have a formula. It's messy, unpredictable, and impossible to control for the shy billionaire inventor and the hockey player who believes he's lost everything.

Moral "Dunny" Dunkirk has a passion for life. A robust outdoorsman, lover of life, and one of the Boston Rebels fan favorites, Dunny has always embraced excitement and the drive to try new things. During his inaugural flight behind the controls of a small plane, the fates decide to test his mettle in a way that he had never envisioned. When everything crashes down around him, he's lost in depression and alone in his cabin, facing an existence that is nothing like the one he previously led. Desperate to find some hope, Dunny reaches out to The Harvey Foundation who might be able to help, and he soon finds himself being lifted out of the pit of darkness he'd fallen into one shy, quirky, uplifting smile at a time.

Accidental billionaire and eccentric inventor Cooper Harvey is only happy in the seclusion of his lab, creating new and wonderful things he is sure will make the world a better place. Other than being blackmailed into spending every fourth Sunday at his PA's house for dinner, he avoids the chaos of the world, and if that means no social life, then he's okay with that. In the most splendid isolation money can buy, he escapes the complicated and difficult emotions surrounding attraction, and his single-minded focus means that sex and love are way down his list. When his latest invention reaches the testing stage, he would normally hand it over to his development team, but a chance meeting with the test subject makes him rethink. Something about the hockey player who'd lost it all makes him think life isn't all about measured chemical reactions, and sometimes it's just about the craziness of love.

Harrisburg Railers

Owatonna U Hockey

Arizona Raptors

Boston Rebels

LA Storm

Chesterford Coyotes - Young Adult

Free Reads

Please note - in all of these free stories, there will be some spoilers for the main series books.

Railers Short Stories

Volume 1 | Volume 2

LA Storm

Sparkle

The Colts - AHL Short Stories

Pucks & Percentages

Breakaway

Making the Save

Standalone

Waiting for Christmas

When hockey wunderkind Tennant Rowe meets his new coach, he knows he's in trouble. Jared Madsen is nine years older than Tennant, impossibly attractive, and — worst of all — his brother's off-limits best friend. Is their chemistry worth the risk?

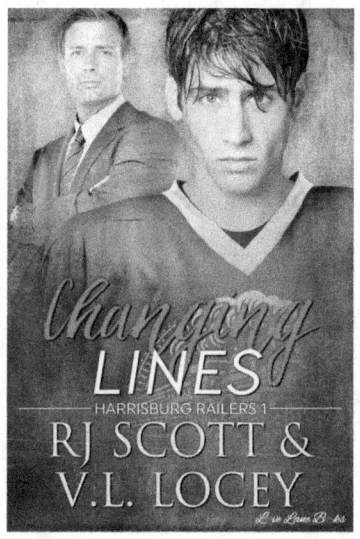

Changing Lines (Railers 1)

Can Tennant show Jared that age is just a number, and that love is all that matters?

The Rowe Brothers are famous hockey hotshots, but as the youngest of the trio, Tennant has always had to play against his brothers' reputations. To get out of their shadows, and against their advice, he accepts a trade to the Harrisburg Railers, where he runs into Jared Madsen. Mads is an old family friend and his brother's one-time teammate. Mads is Tennant's new coach. And Mads is the sexiest thing he's ever laid eyes on.

Jared Madsen's hockey career was cut short by a fault in his heart, but coaching keeps him close to the game. When Ten is traded to the team, his carefully organized world is thrown into chaos. Nine years his junior and his best friend's brother, he knows Ten is strictly off-limits, but as soon as he sees Ten's moves, on and off the ice, he knows that his heart could get him into trouble again.

Changing Lines

Harrisburg Railers (Hockey Romance)

1. Changing Lines
2. First Season
3. Deep Edge
4. Poke Check
5. Last Defense
6. Goal Line
7. Neutral Zone
8. Hat Trick
9. Save The Date
10. Baby Makes Three
11. Rivals
12. Perfect Gifts
13. Family First

Railers Volume 1 | Railers Volume 2 | Railers Volume 3 | Railers Volume 4

Meet the men of Owatonna University's hockey team

Ryker (Owatonna U, 1)

Ryker

Ryker is hockey royalty, Jacob is a poor country boy. Can two vastly different people find common ground and become the men they want to be?

Ryker comes from a long line of championship-winning hockey players. Playing college hockey to develop his game is his only focus, and nothing will stand in the way of him working to become the best player. He has no room for relationships, people who point out his flaws, or anyone who calls him on his dreams. He certainly has no place for love, and meeting Jacob is nothing but a useful distraction on the side. After all trying to get his Owatonna Eagles teammate into bed is less work and more play. When tragedy rocks his family, his charmed life crumbles, and the only person he can turn to is the same one who claims to hate him.

Jacob Benson has only known hard work and stifling conservative values his whole life. Born and raised in the small rural community of Eden Crossing, Minnesota, he's the only son of a hard-working but struggling dairy farming family. Jacob is using his skills in hockey to finance his way to an agricultural science degree. These four years at Owatonna U. will probably be the only time he has to enjoy life, gain acceptance about his sexuality, and live openly before his inevitable return to the farm. Running into a pretty rich boy like Ryker Madsen is putting a damper on his enjoyment of life away from home. Ryker's flip, conceited, carefree attitude grates on Jacob's every nerve. So why, if Ryker is everything he dislikes, does he want nothing more than to explore the sinful dreams that his annoying teammate stars in every night?

Ryker

Owatonna U Hockey (Hockey Romance)

1. Ryker
2. Scott
3. Benoit

4. Christmas Lights
5. Valentine's Hearts
6. Desert Dreams

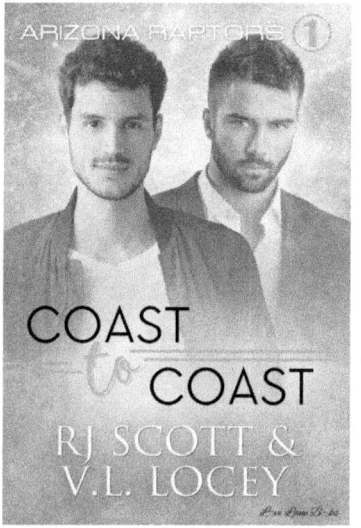

Coast to Coast (Arizona Raptors 1)

Coast To Coast

When opposites attract, this bottom-of-the-league team will never be the same again.

A stipulation in his father's will forces Mark back into the arms of a family that disowned him and leaves him one-third owner of a hockey team facing financial ruin. He doesn't even watch hockey, let alone like it, and wants nothing more than to head back to New York. Then there's the new coach, a stubborn, opinionated, irritating man with superiority issues and questionable music taste. Butting heads with Rowen becomes the new normal, but it comes with passionate debate and an all-consuming lust.

Challenged to rebuild one of the worst teams in the league into a future cup contender, Rowen can't pass up the opportunity. Never in his twenty years of hockey has he ever seen a team managed so badly or coached players overflowing with resentment and bigotry. Yet there's something about this team and this city that compels him to roll up his sleeves and start dismantling. If only Mark, one of three siblings who now own the Raptors, wasn't so damned rock-headed yet so damned appealing his job might be easier. It doesn't look like either is willing to give in, but one night in a dark, desert hotel changes everything.

Coast To Coast

Arizona Raptors (Hockey Romance)

1. Coast To Coast
2. Across the Pond
3. Shadow and Light
4. Sugar and Ice
5. School and Rock

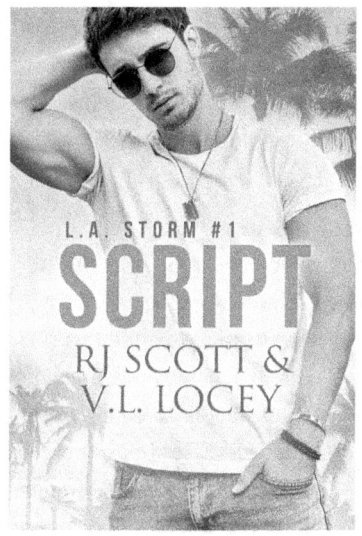

Script (LA Storm, 1)

Script

Hollywood A-lister Finn might be Canadian, but he needs Cameron to show him how to hockey.

Actor Finn Kerrigan is at a crossroads. After growing up a soap star, then starring in a hugely successful trilogy of action movies, he's finally given the chance to read a heartfelt and passionate script that could change his life forever. The role would be enough for people to see him as a serious actor, and maybe even win him an award or two (and no, a golden raspberry award for his action movies doesn't count). Once established as a serious actor he's sure he can come out of the closet and finally live his truth. When he lies to get the part of a hockey player on a struggling team, he suddenly has nowhere to hide. He might be Canadian, but the last time he skated he was ten, and no, he doesn't have hockey in his blood. With only a month until filming starts, he about to be exposed, but partnered with a player who's supposed to be giving him tips, he doesn't realize how many of his secrets will come to light. Falling in lust, one heated kiss at a time, is inevitable, but giving Cameron up at the end of the shoot could break his heart.

Cameron Chavkin is the face of the LA Storm. And the body, and the hair, and the smile. He's at the prime of his career, men and women want to be with him, and he's skating better than he ever has before. His house sits next to a famous rock star's mansion, his garage is filled with expensive cars, and he's even been asked to mentor a once-famous actor in a new hockey movie. Life is pretty sweet. Until the bad boy of hockey meets Finn, a man on the edge with more secrets than Cameron has endorsements.

Knowing better than to get involved, Cameron is swept up despite himself, and when it's time to say goodbye to the Storm's most eligible bachelor is finding it hard to follow the script.

Script

LA Storm

1. Script
2. Second
3. Shield
4. Spiral

Chesterford Coyotes, Young Adult
Romance

Off The Ice (Chesterford Coyotes, 1)

Off The Ice

**A coming-of-age love story with high school, hockey rivalry,
friendship, family, and coming out.**

Soren's life changes in an instant when he and his younger
brother are adopted by hockey royalty. Making sense of his new
life is hard enough, but when he's enrolled in a private school it
means facing a whole new set of problems. Navigating
friendship, family, and hockey is one thing, but being attracted to
the boy who vexes him is a whole new thing.

Felix has a reputation to protect. He's the kid who seems to have everything but looks can be deceiving. Spinning lies about his perfect life, he's created a fantasy world that even he has started to believe. Only, it's not long before everything crumbles, all of his pretty lies are revealed, and only his closest rival sees through his pain and stands by him.

Fighting is easy, friendship is hard, but love is everything.

Off The Ice

Chesterford Coyotes

1. Off The Ice
2. On Thin Ice
3. *Dance on Ice*

Also By RJ Scott

For a full list of ebooks and links please scan the code above or visit rjscott.co.uk/rjbooks

Meet RJ Scott

RJ discovered romance in books at a very young age and realized that if there wasn't romance on the page, she could create it in her head. With over one hundred and fifty books published, she is a full time author of gay romance.

She lives and works out of her home in the beautiful English countryside, spends her spare time reading, watching films, and enjoying time with her family.

The last time she had a week's break from writing she didn't like it one little bit and has yet to meet a box of chocolates she couldn't defeat.

www.rjscott.co.uk | rj@rjscott.co.uk

NEWSLETTER - rjscott.co.uk/rjnews

facebook.com/author.rjscott

x.com/Rjscott_author

instagram.com/rjscott_author

amazon.com/author/rj-scott

bookbub.com/authors/rj-scott

goodreads.com/rjscott

pinterest.com/rjscottauthor

Also By VL Locey

For a full list of ebooks and links please scan the code above or visit vllocey.com/stories-from-vl-locey

Meet V.L. Locey

V.L. Locey loves worn jeans, yoga, belly laughs, walking, reading and writing lusty tales, Greek mythology, the New York Rangers, comic books, and coffee.

(Not necessarily in that order.)

She shares her life with her husband, her daughter, one dog, two cats, a flock of assorted domestic fowl, and two Jersey steers.

When not writing spicy romances, she enjoys spending her day with her menagerie in the rolling hills of Pennsylvania with a cup of fresh java in hand.

vllocey.com
vicki@vllocey.com

Newsletter - vllocey.com/newsletter

facebook.com/V.L.Locey

x.com/vllocey

instagram.com/vl_locey

bookbub.com/authors/v-l-locey

goodreads.com/vllocey

pinterest.com/vllocey